TRANSMIGRATION

TRANSMIGRATION

Nicholas Maes

DUNDURN
TORONTO

Substantive Editor: Niki Chaplin
Copy Editor: Cheryl Hawley
Design: Jennifer Scott
Printer: Webcom

Library and Archives Canada Cataloguing in Publication

Maes, Nicholas, 1960-
    Transmigration / Nicholas Maes.

Issued also in electronic formats.
ISBN 978-1-4597-0231-8

    I. Title.

PS8626.A37T73 2012   jC813'.6   C2011-906603-3

1   2   3   4   5   16   15   14   13   12

We acknowledge the support of the Canada Council for the Arts and the Ontario Arts Council for our publishing program. We also acknowledge the financial support of the Government of Canada through the Canada Book Fund and Livres Canada Books, and the Government of Ontario through the Ontario Book Publishing Tax Credit and the Ontario Media Development Corporation.

Visit us at
Dundurn.com
Definingcanada.ca
@dundurnpress
Facebook.com/dundurnpress

Dundurn	Gazelle Book Services Limited	Dundurn
3 Church Street, Suite 500	White Cross Mills	2250 Military Road
Toronto, Ontario, Canada	High Town, Lancaster, England	Tonawanda, NY
M5E 1M2	LA1 4XS	U.S.A. 14150

To my most beloved homines sapientes,
Deborah, Gershom, Yehuda, and Miriam

Chapter One

Simon could hardly keep himself from yawning. He was waiting by the cash in Noah's Pet Shop for his brother Ian to return from the back. He was tired of apologizing as people brushed by, and of grinning at the cashier who thought he was trying to shoplift. Without knowing it he was staring at a case of vinyl dog bones, his hands in his pockets, a blank look on his face.

After weeks of begging and pleading with his parents, Ian was finally getting a hamster. He was scouting out the choices for the fourth time that week, because he wanted to find a hamster without any flaws. Despite their many trips to the shop, the perfect hamster had eluded him so far.

Simon fidgeted. He had tons of homework to do that evening. He'd been assigned a book report a month before and it was finally due that Friday. He hadn't even started reading the novel. There was a math test too, the very next day, and while math was one of his better subjects, his attention had been slackening these last few weeks. It was the same with biology: he had a project due on evolution and so far he hadn't lifted a finger. So why was he wasting time in that shop? His best bet was to track Ian down and drag him away, by force if necessary, even if he had to traipse to the back where music was blaring from a half-dozen speakers. He was preparing himself for the gruelling ordeal when he heard a familiar voice call out, "Well, look who's here."

Simon wheeled and practically groaned. Confronting him were Winston and Peter, the coolest kids in his grade eleven homeroom. Peter's dad was a hotshot lawyer, and Winston's owned half of Chinatown. Handsome, athletic, popular, and rich, the pair had more than their share of good luck. So why did hipsters like them love to pick on Simon? It was funny, in a sick sort of way. The moment they caught sight of him, they would drop everything (unless they were playing online poker) and follow him all over the place, like dogs in hot pursuit of a chicken.

"You can't say hello?" Peter demanded. Even though he was born in Vancouver, he had a slight South African accent.

"He's pretending he doesn't know us," Winston said, his smile mocking and faintly cruel. With his sleek frame and sinewy limbs, he resembled a fighter in a Kung Fu film. And he *was* extremely quick on his feet, maybe because he took Ritalin daily. "He's ashamed to be seen with us. We're not cool enough for a guy like him."

"I was thinking about something."

"About those dog bones, right?" Peter jeered with a malicious smile.

"What?"

"You seem to be eyeing those bones real closely. I guess your dog has exacting tastes."

"I'm waiting for my brother."

"A brother? Really? Is he from the shallow end of the gene pool too?" Peter was smirking. He was having fun.

"If you say so."

"Carpenter, there's no point riding you if you won't fight back." Like Peter, Winston was smiling widely. Simon practically groaned. These guys were getting started and wouldn't leave him alone — unless he managed to distract them somehow.

"You'd better hurry. The snakes are getting ready to eat."

"What do you mean?" Peter's smirk faded slightly.

"You're here to watch the snakes, right? The staff is getting ready to feed them."

"How do you know? The snakes are at the back."

"Because the mice are panicked," Simon said. "They sense what's coming and are squeaking in fear."

"Are you saying you can hear them?" Winston asked scornfully.

"You can't?" Simon was surprised. It amazed him how dull people's senses could be. The mice were so panicked that their squeaking was awful — and that was with the music blasting.

"Of course we hear them," Peter lied. "And that means the show's about to begin. I guess we'll catch you later, eh? Come on, Win. Let's leave genius here to study his dog bones."

As the pair moved off, Simon called to them, "If you see my brother, can you tell him I'm waiting?"

"What am I? A messenger service? Go tell him yourself!" Peter yelled back.

"Go to hell, Carpenter!" Winston added.

They passed down an aisle. Winston announced, in a very loud voice, that Simon was the weirdest kid in school, "Grade A weird," he practically shouted. "One day we'll read he's some psycho killer."

If their purpose was to worry Simon, they'd achieved their goal. He knew he was weird in everyone's eyes. His very family thought he was strange, his mom, dad, and even Ian. "The eccentric," they called him, in a friendly way. His parents would often throw him this look when they learned that he'd neglected to study or became distracted when driving the car. If he really was "eccentric," as his family believed, then Winston was right and he was possibly psycho.

But there he was, worrying again. He'd promised himself he wouldn't dwell on this stuff and go back to acting like the kid he'd been four years ago. Until his thirteenth birthday he'd been normal enough and people like Winston would never …

Winston. If that oaf came back and found him standing by the dog bones, he would make Simon's life hell, there and in school. Simon had to grab his brother and leave. Now, while the going was good. Why did he keep stalling?

As if he didn't know.

To begin with, the store's lighting was horrible. The

fluorescent bulbs were like fire on his eyes and their drone-like hum was driving him crazy. The towering shelves were boxing him in, as were the pets in their stainless-steel cages — what person in his right mind would keep an animal trapped?

But the worst part was the music. There were speakers hanging all over the place. The further you went the more the music lunged at you. Simon loathed it more than he could say. The mix of high- and low-pitched notes felt like vicious pinpricks against his skull, and the faster they sounded the more pain they inflicted, until his head was on the verge of exploding. And as soon as one song finished another would begin, and the agony would start all over again.

"It depends on the music," his dad once said, when Simon had complained about a radio blaring. "Some music is awful, sure. Like that hop hip stuff ..."

"Hip hop," Ian had corrected him.

"But there's jazz, baroque, classical, and folk. There's something for everyone, that's what I'm saying."

He was wrong. All music made Simon want to puke. Not metaphorically (as his dad would say), but actually puke. He wondered why people sought this torture out, carrying iPods around to fill their heads with poison. And why would stores pump this garbage out day and night, indifferent to the misery they caused? Music should be outlawed, he thought. Just like people couldn't carry guns, it should be illegal to play music in public.

This wasn't helping any. He still had tons of homework to do and Ian was drooling over the hamsters.

Enough was enough. Simon would use brute force and yank him away. Otherwise he'd stay until the staff kicked him out, admiring one ball of fur after the next. And, again, if Winston found him there …

Simon gritted his teeth and rushed down an aisle. He hurried past the avian section, with its finches, budgies, and a sad looking parrot; then came the aquaria, with its fish swimming blindly in circles, goldfish, angel fish, guppies, and loaches; then there were the puppies, the ferrets, cats, gerbils, mice, and …

He stopped.

Behind the music — which sounded like people being beaten to death — some poor soul was screaming. The voice was odd, not like any he'd heard. Its timbre was rough and the pitch was different, less controlled … not quite human. It sounded like a bird was peeping, a squirrel was maybe clearing its throat, and air was leaving a balloon. For all its strangeness and frailty, however, there was no mistaking the rage it projected. It contained a furious, violent note.

"… Who de hell d'you think you are, jailin' me like dis! Let me outta here! And turn dat crappy music off! If you don't let me out, I'll break out on my own. And when I'm free, you *lura* oafs, I'll cut your stinkin' throats!"

Simon's blood turned cold. The sound was coming from up ahead, near a stack of cages that contained all sorts of rabbits. Was someone trapped inside? No, how could that be? Who could fit inside a cage so small?

"Did you hear me? I said I'll cut your throats!"

Even as he trembled slightly, Simon did feel sorry

for this stranger. He glanced up and down the shelves, desperate to help the poor guy out. Slowly a realization dawned: no one else noticed the shouting. The staff and customers weren't batting an eye, as if it were normal for someone to be shrieking like that.

Hang on a sec! What was *that*?

To his right was a rectangular cage, three feet long and two feet wide. It had a clear plastic lid with metal mesh on top. Inside, beside a wooden hut, a Mini Rex rabbit twitched its nose. It was grey, white, and innocent looking. Its ears were downy and pink on the inside, it had a blood-red stain on its right front paw, and its eyes were two pure ebony marbles. It looked like any common rabbit but … those shouts and curses? They were coming from *it*. Simon crouched, just to be sure. Yep. A rabbit, a *rabbit*, was muttering threats. He stared at it dumbstruck.

"What the hell'r you lookin' at? You ain't seen a rabbit before, you fat, ugly *lura*?"

"What? Wait. Are you talking to me?" The hair on Simon's neck was bristling.

"Yeah, I'm talkin' to you! Hey! Dis is somethin'! Can you actually hear me? I mean, no joke, I'm gettin' through to you?"

"Is this some type of trick?" Simon glanced around nervously, thinking Winston was behind this "talking" creature. He was good with tech stuff and had maybe hidden a device in the cage. That was it. Winston was talking into a nearby mike and capturing Simon's response on film. He would screen it in school and Simon would look like a fool.

"It ain't no trick!" the voice continued. The rabbit had its paws against the lid, in what seemed to be a show of desperation. "But you ain't answered me! How come you can hear me? Who de hell are you?"

"So you're not Winston?"

"Who de hell's Winston? Look, dis is amazin'. I don't know who you are, but I can tell one thing: you don't know who you are either, not if you're receivin' me. But never mind. Dat's okay. The point is, I need help. You gotta open dis cage and let me go. Better yet, take me home. I swear to youse on all dat's holy, you help me out and I'll pay you back …"

"Simon!" Much to Simon's relief, Ian appeared. "I'm ready to go. I finally found the perfect hamster. The clerk, his name's Tim, said he'll put him aside. We can pick him up tomorrow, or the next day, even. What's wrong? Your face is really pale."

"Nothing," Simon said, eyeing the rabbit still. "What do you make of this rabbit? Does he seem normal?"

"The rabbit? Yeah, he's normal enough. Although he's nothing like Magnus."

"Magnus?"

"My hamster. That salesman, Tim, said Magnus is special. You should see the way he ate some apple …"

"Hey!" the rabbit interrupted, "did you hear what I said? Help me and I'll pay you back."

"Did you hear that?" Simon asked.

"What? The music? Or that parrot squawking?"

"Yeah, the parrot," Simon said. He tried to smile but it looked like a grimace.

"What's the matter?"

"Nothing. Look, we should go. We've been here half an hour already and I have a massive test tomorrow." He turned and led Ian away.

"Hey! You can't leave!" the rabbit screamed. "All I'm asking is you open dis cage!"

"Let's go!" Simon insisted, picking up his pace.

"Come back! Help me! I'll kick your head in if you don't!"

Simon bolted toward the exit. With every step the rabbit's cursing grew fainter, until it vanished altogether as Simon passed into the late spring air. He was sweating heavily and his legs were shaking. Luckily, Ian was too happy to notice. He was talking about Magnus and how he was the world's smartest hamster. To shut him up, Simon offered to race. Ian liked racing, especially when Simon let him win.

"You were probably dreaming," he told himself as he and Ian started running down the sidewalk.

But it was no dream. Either that rabbit had spoken or, like Winston said, he was totally nuts.

Chapter Two

The brothers raced for several blocks until they reached their street in the heart of South Cambie. Slowing to a walk, Ian declared himself the victor. Simon merely nodded. Winning meant a lot to Ian, whereas he didn't care. And it was beautiful out. The wind was causing the trees to rustle. The late spring air, the sinking sun, and his exhilarating run had allowed Simon to forget about Winston and Peter — and that "talking" rabbit. It would rain soon, his instincts told him, and there was nothing better than a cleansing cloudburst. Chicks were nesting in a nearby tree. His nose told him Ms. Fields was cooking stew and that Jimmy, her son, badly needed to shower. He could smell something else. It was over in some bushes.

"Careful," he told Ian who was walking ahead, "there's a raccoon in that hedge to your left."

"I don't see him," Ian said.

"He's eating garbage."

"I don't see it," Ian repeated. Thinking Simon was trying to scare him, he took a run at the hedge. A grey shape exploded from inside and loped across the road, a bone in its mouth.

"I told you. And Henry's back."

Between the Carpenter house and the next door neighbour's was an unpaved alley steeped in shadow. It was overgrown with weeds and ferns, blocked to traffic, and generally unused. A bum named Henry would sleep there in a makeshift shelter, usually after drinking himself stupid. He was harmless and residents let him be.

"Hey, Henry!" Ian called. "I'm getting a hamster!"

"He's out cold," Simon said, flinching at the smell of whisky.

"Why does he drink?" Ian asked, stooping over the middle-aged man. He passed a hand over his eyes but got no reaction.

"Because he feels out of place, I guess. The whisky makes him think he belongs."

"That's projection, isn't it?"

"Projection?"

"You feel out of place. I heard you say as much to dad. So you're projecting your feelings onto Henry, see?"

"So you think I'm going to end up like this?"

"Maybe. I don't know. Let's plan to bring Magnus home tomorrow?"

As Ian described his hamster's good looks, Simon mulled his statement over. Yes, he did feel out of place. When he compared himself to Winston, say, he felt like an outdated piece of equipment. If Winston was the newest 4G cellphone, Simon was the ancient rotary model, clumsy, immobile, and no longer in use. Everything about him …

His train of thought was interrupted. Inside his skull a switch was being thrown — at least, that's what it felt like. As he and Ian walked away from Henry, their backs fully turned on his sprawled figure, for a fleeting instant Simon could *see* them moving away, could see Ian waving his arms and his own frame bobbing as he ambled forward. As if he were seeing things through Henry's eyes. He blinked in surprise and his view returned to normal.

What the…?

"You're not listening," Ian said.

"No."

"In that case, forget it. Magnus deserves better than that."

Ian ran to their porch and passed inside. Feeling bad that he'd upset his brother — Ian got angry when people didn't listen — Simon paused and studied their home.

It was a two-storey house with a black slate roof, four bay windows, and Grecian pillars flanking the door. It was an ordinary residence, not too big and not too small, with just enough space (now that the attic had been altered) for all four Carpenters and their live-in nanny. The furnishings were nice — his parents earned good money — but Simon didn't care much for the designer couches, granite counters, and stainless-steel fridge. In his opinion their home's best feature was the fact that happy people had lived there always, for the sixty odd years that it had been standing. He'd mentioned this to the family once, only to trigger a question from Ian: how could he know the former tenants had been happy and no murderers or madmen had been hidden among them? "You can feel it in the walls," Simon had said, matter-of-factly.

There *was* one exception and that person was Simon; only he was more frustrated than sad. And he hadn't always been frustrated either. When he'd been younger, things had been great. In grade three he'd been a number-one speller; in grade four he'd won a school-wide contest; in grade seven he'd been dubbed "junior tech whiz" in Vancouver, beating out some stiff competition. Again and again his dad had predicted that Simon would become an engineer like him.

But then, in grade eight, there had been the "incident." It had been a rainy day in March. Simon had been delivering papers on a nearby street. One house was guarded by a Doberman pinscher that was tied to the porch by a ten-foot rope. The dog was a mean one, to judge by its barking, never mind that its owner swore that Thor was kind and even-tempered. If that were so, why had it lunged at Simon, barking and slathering spit all over? And when the rope had slipped and freed the brute, why had it made a beeline for Simon, growling and baring its three-inch fangs?

There were two versions of what happened next. According to the accepted one, the fiend had jumped at Simon and he'd struck his head on a stone. The proof was the paw marks on Simon's pants and jacket.

The second version — which people didn't know

— was that a "switch" in Simon's brain had engaged and he'd felt he was inside the dog. Both Simon and Thor had been deeply shocked and that's when the dog had taken a run at his body, as if to deliver Simon back to himself, banging him against the stone in the process. In the seconds that had followed, Thor had stared into his eyes, in an effort to help, not to do him harm.

One way or another, Simon's head had been injured. When his mother had found out she'd inspected him closely — she was a pediatrician at the Children's Hospital. X-rays were taken, neurologists had probed him, a psychiatrist had barraged him with useless questions — did he love his parents? did he like setting fires? — and a battery of tests had duly followed, most involving lights being shined into his eyes. There'd been no damage found, apart from a concussion. But from that point on, his course was downhill.

Slowly he'd grown more distracted. Once sharp, focused, and on the ball, he would stare into space, neglect certain tasks, or unexpectedly tune out altogether. When he wasn't driving his parents crazy, he would fill them with concern.

His dad had stopped saying that he would become an engineer.

Music had started driving him nuts. Until then, he hadn't minded the Beatles or the odd symphony his dad would put on. But after? The sounds had shredded his nerves, to the point he would moan in pain and come close to puking.

"Why are you outside? It's starting to rain."

Simon started, then realized it was Emma speaking. She was their live-in nanny and had been with the family as long as he remembered. As she'd told him many times before, he'd seen her face before anyone else's.

It was funny. He'd heard the story of his birth so often that he could picture it almost. A month before her due date, his mom had been driving and crashed into a lamppost. It had been late at night and the streets had been empty. The collision must have jarred something loose, breaking her water and starting contractions, painful ones at frequent intervals, a sign the baby was coming fast. Shocked and bruised and bleeding from her forehead, she'd forgotten all her medical skills and sat there helplessly, clueless what to do.

By chance, Emma had happened along — Simon pictured her running with that funny stride of hers. Realizing this lady was about to give birth, she'd calmed her down, delivered the baby, cut the cord, and wrapped the newborn in a sweater — Simon could feel its prickles against his skin.

In the days that followed, Emma had stopped by often and helped his mother care for the baby. Hearing the Carpenters were looking for a nanny, Emma had applied for the job and, from that day on, had been part of the family.

Simon knew her better than he did his mom. His parents had jobs that pushed them hard and forced them to work the craziest hours. They would often come home late at night, only to leave at dawn the next morning. While he and Ian had outgrown a nanny, his parents would never get rid of Emma because the family would have been lost without her.

That said, she was a bit of a puzzle. Apart from her daughter, Clara, she had no relatives or friends. Sometimes she'd get a letter in the mail — the handwriting on it was always the same — but she never said who the writer was and only smiled when the family spoke of her "boyfriend."

She also drank, Simon knew. This didn't happen often; in fact, she only drank when she visited her daughter, to fortify her nerves, and who could blame her? His parents didn't know and Simon wasn't going to tell them.

"Don't just stand there. Come inside and I'll brew you some tea."

"I was checking up on Henry," Simon spoke as he climbed the porch and followed Emma to the kitchen.

"Have you seen my necklace?" she inquired, entering the kitchen and switching on the kettle.

"No. You were wearing it at breakfast," he said, sitting at a table.

"I took it off and can't remember where I put it. Never mind. It will turn up later. So tell me about your day."

"There's not much to report."

"There must be something," she insisted in an attempt to draw him out. When Simon's parents discussed his mental state, she unfailingly argued that he would come into his own. If not for her, he would have lost all hope.

"I got two quizzes back, in French and chemistry."

"How did they go?"

"So so."

"You'll do better next time. Anything else?"

"That's it."

"You can do better than that. I seldom leave the house, and rely on you to bring me gossip."

"Okay. A rabbit spoke to me."

He hadn't intended to mention the rabbit, but the words slipped out. He didn't think she would notice much and was surprised when she glanced at him sharply.

While not an ugly woman, she was certainly no knockout. She wasn't tall and her build was stocky, with square shoulders, wide hips, and small, solid hands. She was as strong as a horse — she'd once lifted a trunk that both his parents couldn't budge. Her face was squat, her cheekbones wide, and her jaw outsized and a bit ungainly. Her hair was coarse and reddish brown, while her eyes were a beautiful coral colour with depths that seemed to fall forever. They were especially intense now because his remark had upset her.

"A rabbit spoke? What do you mean? Where did this happen? What did it say?"

"Emma," he said quietly, deciding to kill the subject, "I was only joking."

She stared at him fiercely then burst out laughing. Placing a tea bag in an oversized mug — on it was written GENIUS AT WORK — she took the kettle that had boiled by now and filled the cup just short of the brim, commenting she was foolish for thinking an animal could speak.

Simon moved to a different topic. "How's Clara?"

"She's fine. I'm going to visit her tomorrow. Want to tag along?"

"Sure. I'll buy her an Oh Henry! bar."

Again Emma surprised him. Turning from the kettle, she hugged him fiercely. Just as quickly she returned to his tea, adding milk and plenty of sugar.

"What was that for?" he asked.

"Because you're always kind to her."

Clara was Simon's age and badly autistic. Her state was so severe that she passed all her days in a Vancouver Heights home, along with other troubled children. From the time when he was little, Emma had taken Simon to visit Clara and, while the home was depressing, Simon had come to like her. She never said a word — this was part of her condition — but there was something oddly calm about her and Simon felt at peace when he was seated beside her. Over the last three years this impression had grown; whereas he often felt uncomfortable and out of place, Clara strangely set him at ease.

Emma was delighted that they'd hit it off. The only time she'd been taken aback was when he'd asked her about Clara's father. She'd answered tersely that her ex had been difficult and Simon had never raised the subject again.

"Your driving instructor phoned," Emma said, handing him his tea. "He wanted to know if you're still taking lessons. I said I wasn't sure."

"You should've told him I'm not ready to drive, according to my father."

"It would sound a lot better coming from you."

Simon sipped his tea. He and his dad had gone driving last week. While Simon handled the car well enough, he had a habit of making unpredictable turns and his dad didn't like it. When asked why he drove in this erratic fashion, switching lanes and veering onto side streets, Simon said he was choosing the fastest route. When asked how he could know this route was the fastest, Simon always answered that he somehow did. The alternative was to explain that sometimes he saw the city laid before him, together with its traffic flow. Last week when he'd changed lanes unexpectedly and his dad had spilled his coffee all over? He'd done that to avoid a crash ahead. But his manoeuvre had been the very last straw. His dad had said he wasn't focused enough.

"Does Ian like onions?" Emma asked, bringing him back to the kitchen. "I always forget."

"No. He found a hamster, incidentally."

"It's about time. Who'll clean the cage?"

"That'll be my job."

"Or mine most likely."

Smiling, Simon sipped his tea. The rain had started and the windows were streaming, a sight that always picked him up. The sound of Emma grating cheese was soothing and the tensions from the day were starting to ebb. The steam from his tea was spiralling upward and his eyes were getting heavy. From far away he felt that sensation again, of a switch inside his head being thrown.

An instant later he was level with the ceiling. He could see Emma working and his body slouched at the table. The room was spread before him, the countertop, the gas stove, the cupboards, the ingredients for that night's supper. And to their left, on top of the fridge, he spied a wicker basket. In it was a necklace …

The front door banged. His mother was home. Simon started from his reverie. For a moment he marvelled at the details in the dream, the way they matched the setup in the kitchen. His mother called hello. He got up to greet her. Pausing at the door, he considered the fridge. His mother called again. He could hear Ian telling her all about Magnus. Emma yelled hello. Frowning slightly, Simon approached the fridge and felt its top with his fingertips. They encountered a basket. And inside?

His entire body tingled as his fingers closed on Emma's necklace.

Chapter Three

"Soon after *On the Origin of Species* appeared, Herbert Spencer coined the phrase 'survival of the fittest,' which he used to summarize Darwin's theory. Based on what we've seen today, can you tell me why he isn't doing any justice to Darwin?"

Simon was in his biology class, staring at the floor. He wished his teacher would stop droning on. For an hour she'd been talking about evolution, with endless references to birds, bugs, and degrees of variation. While nature normally held his interest, this talk of adaptation had him feeling queasy.

"… What is Spencer saying? He believes there are traits that, on their own, make some men superior to others. He thinks that whites, for example, are better than everyone else, that it's always preferable to have white skin and blue eyes. This wasn't Darwin's point of view. He would agree white skin is sometimes an advantage, in northern Europe say, but that black skin would be 'better' in sunnier climates …"

Simon's eyes were closed and he seemed to be dozing, but in actual fact he was focusing hard. His nerves were stretched taut. He felt like someone clinging to a cliff who could fall to the rocks below at any moment. It was lucky they had an early closing that day and he could leave as soon as the lunch bell rang.

"… Let's talk about the peppered moth. There are white ones and black ones. Both nest on trees with a light-coloured bark. In early times the white ones were hard to spot, while the black ones were easy. Predators caught more black than white, and this meant 'white' was 'better,' while 'black' was not. When industry grew the trees became sooty, and the white stood out more than the black. So 'white' became a handicap and 'black' an advantage. You see? The environment determines what works and what doesn't. One trait can beat its rival for awhile, but there are times when the rival will barrel forward. Nothing stands still. Nothing's written in stone."

Something was different. On awakening that morning, Simon felt something had changed. The walls in his room, the floor, and ceiling seemed to meet at uneven angles, and the effect had left him feeling unbalanced. His body was more alien than normal: it seemed to fit him (whatever that meant) like a fat man's shirts and pants on a beanpole. His bones felt heavy, as if the marrow was leaden, his eyes were wobbly and his fingers tingled.

And what about his senses? They were on a hair-trigger like never before. Every noise was like a shout in his ear, his eyes could see with deadly clarity, and his nose was catching everything, everything. That morning, as he'd lain in bed, he'd smelled his dad's aftershave from one floor up, a mint that was trapped between two floorboards, and the acrid scent of cheap cigars from a tenant who'd lived in their house years earlier.

In class, Joy Fung had cherry gum in her purse, Meryl Fluting had used a peach shampoo, Mike Potts had socks that needed changing, and Sherkhan, the janitor's cat, had eaten tuna.

"Excuse me, Simon. This isn't your bedroom ..."

More than anything, the noise threw him off. It was a static-like buzz echoing deep inside him, like he was in a stadium and hearing a crowd yell. This wall of sound was driving him crazy.

Crazy. Yes. He was losing his mind.

"Simon! Wake up! We have work to do!"

"Sorry. What was that, Ms. Guzman?" Simon answered groggily, his black-ringed eyes opening slowly. The teacher was standing directly beside him.

"Have you heard a single word I've said?"

"About evolution? I heard everything."

"Really? So summarize the theory of Natural Selection."

"Animals change because of their surroundings. Some traits are more useful than others but this can change if the environment's altered."

"Good."

"Because this process lasts forever, we could one day disappear."

"Pardon me?"

"Humans have rivals too. Something new can appear or something old could take over."

Nicholas Maes

"Anything is possible," she said with a laugh, "but I wouldn't worry too much about cavemen returning."

Much to Simon's relief the bell suddenly rang. Ms. Guzman turned away from him and advised the class to read chapter four at home. Simon was in the hall already, racing toward the exit. They had a short recess and if he left for some air he might calm his nerves a little. Once outside he would walk to a park, lie on the grass, and close his eyes. Never mind he had that math test later.

"Hey, Dog Bone!"

Oh no. Peter and Winston were blocking his path. It was funny how much they resembled each other, although Winston was Chinese and Peter was white. It wasn't just their clothes — they were dressed in match-ing shirts and pants — but their faces as well. Both had a lean, wolf-like look, as well as the same mocking smile.

"How's it going, Dog Bone?"

"Why are you calling me Dog Bone?"

"Because we saw you in the pet shop, remember?"

"Yeah. So?"

"So you were looking for a bone to give your brother."

"I was waiting for him to choose a hamster."

"It didn't look that way to us." Winston was smirking. Eyeing him, Simon was almost drowned in impressions. His aftershave was strong, as was the smell of cigarettes, and his hands were shaking, from his Ritalin no doubt. But it was strange. He was usually confident but now there was a gap, as if his typical hard demeanour had cracked a little. For a moment, Simon felt a surge and a hiss burst about him. Just as quickly it died away.

"I'm sorry your mother's sick," he said.

It was as if he'd doused Winston with a bucket of water. His smile melted and a look of fury appeared.

"Number one, she isn't sick," he fumed. "And number two, it isn't your business. What are you up to? Are you stalking me?"

"What are you talking about? Who's a stalker?" Simon asked.

"Is your mom really sick, man?" Peter broke in.

"My mom's not sick!" Winston yelled, lunging forward and shoving Simon. "The tests mean nothing!"

"I'm glad," Simon said, with a shaky smile.

"… And this is what you get for stalking me!"

Winston was going to give him a kick. He'd assumed a fighting stance and was lifting his foot. Before he could strike, he was pushed from behind. He stumbled, swore, and faced the intruder. When he saw who it was, he took a step back.

Facing him was Jenny Frobisher. Apart from Simon, she was the strangest kid in school. The rumour was she was at least nineteen and had failed three grades over the last six years. Short but powerful, with russet hair and green eyes, she roamed the hallways silently, a lot like Sherkhan. She made Simon nervous because she seemed very tough.

Winston felt it too. His eyes were spitting hate but her presence reined him in. He tried to shake his torpor but he couldn't attack, as if a powerful hand were holding him back. He turned and motioned Peter to follow, saying they just had time to play some poker online.

Warning Simon they would catch him later, they saun-
tered off.

"Thank you," Simon said, when Winston had gone.
"For some strange reason, the guy really hates me."

Jenny Frobisher stared at him. Her eyes were like
a pair of blinding searchlights. Without warning she
grabbed his wrist — she moved so quickly that he
couldn't avoid her. She held it for an instant then let it
drop. A moment later she was walking off, as if respond-
ing to a summons only she could hear.

Simon sighed. His head was killing him and his
nerves were ringing, but for the first time that morning
he felt a bit better.

"Hello, Clara. I'm here. And look who's with me. It's your
good friend Simon."

Emma stooped and kissed her daughter, who was
seated at a desk before a large picture window. It looked
north onto the Burrard Inlet. The sun was setting and
wisps of fog were drifting in. There wasn't much wind
and the water on the inlet looked unusually still, as if
it were setting a trap or something. She and Simon sat
next to Clara.

As soon as he'd arrived home from school, Emma
had said she was off to see Clara and asked if he would
join her still. In need of a distraction, he'd said yes. After
stopping off in a variety store, where he'd purchased an
Oh Henry!, they'd taken a bus to Brentwood Station,
transferred at Willingdon near the tech institute, and

headed north to Confederation Park and the Sarah Dooley Home for Children. Except for some music at large, the ride had been pleasant.

Emma *did* comment that Simon seemed restless. He explained that he'd had some coffee at lunch and the caffeine was making him antsy still. There was no point telling her how weird he felt or about his showdown with Winston that morning. The same way he wouldn't mention that, as always happened when they dropped in on Clara, Emma had been boozing it up. After all, she was in a great mood. She'd received a letter from her "boyfriend" that morning and through the length of the bus ride had read it over with gusto. Who was this guy?

"The sea looks beautiful," Emma went on, stroking Clara's shoulder. "Although I wish it were storming. I love it when the waves take shape and crash against the rocks on shore. What about that chocolate, Simon?"

"Right," he said, taking the candy from his pocket. He put it on the desk and took several steps back, aware that Clara fidgeted when people got near. "I hope you like Oh Henry! still."

She took the chocolate without saying a word. Simon didn't mind, as he knew she never spoke. She behaved the exact same way with her mother, never speaking and never kissing her back. Emma had never said as much, but her daughter was a mute.

On the other hand, she had surprising talents. Two years ago a bird had flown into a window and broken both its wings. The resident doctor knew something about birds and had taken time to examine the sparrow, only to conclude it couldn't be saved. That's when Clara had intervened, taking the bird into her care. Within days it was healed. And a year ago a nurse had cut her hand badly, severing the artery beside her thumb. She might have lost consciousness if not for Clara. The doctor couldn't explain it to this day, but she'd somehow managed to staunch the blood.

"Let me help you with the chocolate, sweet. The wrapping's hard to tear. Would you like a piece, Simon?"

"No thanks. I'm fine."

Settling back, he studied mother and daughter. They looked a lot alike: both were short, had red wiry hair, and the exact same coral eyes. Like her mother, Clara projected great strength and would pace for hours in the downstairs gym — she never walked outside. Once she'd lifted one of the guards, a big man weighing at least a hundred kilos. And she rarely slept, according to the doctors. Two hours was all she needed, and she would get this in snatches, minutes here, minutes there.

Still, despite her talents and natural strength, her mind wasn't normal. Not only was she silent but her stare was peculiar. It wasn't blank — there was a great depth to it — but it was directed inward, as if the world didn't interest her. At the same time, her posture was impossibly straight and suggested someone who was on the alert, who was listening for sounds of a possible intruder. Maybe that was why she slept so poorly.

Overall, Simon liked her. He always felt relaxed in her presence, because she never cared if he spoke or not. No, it was more than that: he felt restored when he was with her, less bothered and more confident. For the first time since he'd awakened that morning, his nerves weren't strained and the static had grown silent. Emma was happy to do the talking and described her morning routines, the cleaning, cooking, and grocery shopping. Clara was drawing with a pad and coloured pencils.

Her fingers moved decisively and with practised swiftness. After maybe ten minutes one drawing was done. While nicely executed, it wasn't easy to make sense of. The swirls of colour depicted a cave, with stalactites and stalagmites and four large boulders forming a table. This cave stood next to the sea, to judge by a series of squiggles in the background and the scene of a shark chasing after a fish.

As Clara touched her drawing up, Emma said she'd speak to Dr. Brown, the institute's psychiatrist. Simon shrugged. Emma always saw the doctor on her visits, to check up on her daughter's progress — or lack thereof. When her mother left the room, Clara began a second drawing.

Simon stared at the flattened sea. Its tint was deepening as the sun sank lower. His thoughts were wandering. His nerves weren't nearly as unsettled now, but he wondered why he'd felt on edge to begin with, why his head was full of voice-like static, and why his senses were so finely honed — he could smell meat cooking in the building's kitchen, which was at least four storeys down in the basement. This wasn't normal. And why had he mentioned Winston's mother? How had he known she was sick when he'd never even met her before?

Minutes passed as he continued brooding. He was on the verge of nodding off, exhausted by his worries, when Clara's movements startled him awake. He eyed her drawings, then sat up in his chair. What the…?

She'd finished three sketches and laid them in a row. The first showed shadows flying in a mass, like a flock of birds or swarm of ghosts. There were hundreds of them, thousands, all trapped (it seemed) in a human body. While the picture was a simple sketch, it shimmered with emotion, most notably fear.

The second was much eerier. It showed two figures sitting arm-in-arm. One was normal and looked like Clara, while the other was ghost-like and floating off. The feeling it projected was one of desperate sadness.

But the last sketch was shocking. Eyeing it, he blanched and jumped to his feet. His head was pounding and his palms felt damp.

"How did you know?" he finally spoke.

Clara didn't answer. She was busy putting her pencils away. As soon as she'd tidied them, she stood and walked toward a nearby door. Halfway there, she returned to the desk: she'd forgotten to take her chocolate with her. Grabbing this, she struggled a moment then finally spoke a single word: "*Woplh.*"

"*Woplh,*" she repeated, with a very great effort. This said, she turned and drifted past the doorway.

Left on his own, Simon stared at the drawing. It showed a cage with a transparent lid and a metal mesh on top. Inside the cage was a grey and white rabbit. Its eyes were firmly fastened on Simon and its mouth was open, as if it were speaking.

That static sound was louder than ever and his nerves felt strained to the point of tearing. As he struggled to contain his fear, he wondered why she'd drawn the rabbit with a pair of vicious fangs.

Chapter Four

It was 5:41 p.m. when Simon got home. Emma offered him a cup of tea but he said no thanks and raced upstairs. Entering his room, he emptied out his piggy bank. He stuffed his pockets with bills and change, hurried downstairs, and left the house. He didn't stop running until he reached Noah's Pet Shop. It was scheduled to close at six and he'd made it with just minutes to spare.

He hurried to the rabbit aisle and searched the section frantically. There were white ones, black ones, grey ones, and a Mini Rex, but the talking one with the stain on its paw was nowhere to be seen. Had someone bought it earlier that day? Sickened by the music playing, he ran to the back and scanned the various cages.

"We're closing in three minutes," a clerk announced. He had dyed black hair and studs in his lips. "If you're buying something, bring it to the cash. Otherwise I'm gonna have to kick you out."

"There was a Mini Rex rabbit with a stain on its paw. But I can't see him."

"I don't keep track of the rabbits we sell. And there are plenty of others …"

"It's got to be this one. Please. It's urgent."

"Hey, Sarah!" the clerk yelled, eyeing Simon as if he were nuts. "Do you know about a Mini Rex with a stain on its paw? Some guy here says it's an emergency."

"Monster Bugs?" a girl replied, appearing from the rear. She was holding a cockatoo and stroking its feathers. There was a leather strap on one of its legs and attached to it was a delicate chain.

"Monster Bugs?" Simon asked.

"As in 'Monster Bugs Bunny,'" Sarah replied. "That's one tough rabbit you're interested in."

"Did you sell it? I can't see …"

"Are you kidding? Three customers complained it was possessed or something. I thought they were crazy but it freaked me out too —" She broke off as the cockatoo shrieked.

"That strap's too tight," Simon observed.

"What'd you say?" Sarah asked, stroking the bird in an effort to calm it. Its shrieking continued.

"That strap," Simon said, "it's chaffing the bird's leg."

"How do you know?" the cool guy yawned.

"I don't know. I just do," Simon replied. He shivered visibly. The background music was rubbing him raw.

"Look," the guy said, "it's getting late. We're closing in three minutes so …"

"He's right," Sarah spoke, inspecting the band, "the

band's too snug. Take Buddy to his cage and adjust it, will you? In the meantime," she told Simon, "I'll show you your rabbit."

They entered a storage space way at the back. It contained aquaria full of crickets and snails — food for the snakes and lizards around them. Simon felt bad for these bugs and was thinking how brutal nature was, the way it sets creatures eating each other.

"There he is," Sarah cried, motioning to a cage in a distant corner. Inside it was a Mini Rex eating an apple. Simon saw the stain on its paw.

"That's him all right."

"So? Do you want him? You've gotta make up your mind."

Simon hardly heard her. He was eyeing the rabbit. It was eating the apple and seemed pretty normal. The idea of it talking struck Simon as crazy. After all, how could such an animal speak? It had no larynx, its brain was too small, and ...

He almost gasped with relief. His nerves were strained, the music was horrible, his head ached like crazy, but this rabbit hadn't talked to him at least. It was one less thing to worry about. His mouth was open to thank the girl and to tell her he wouldn't be needing the rabbit, when a wheedling voice leapt out at him. "I just about gave up on you. It's good you're here. Dat music's killin' me."

His mouth dropped open as he stared at the creature. It nibbled the apple and showed no sign of having spoken.

"You takin' me home?" it went on, giving him a side-ways glance. "That *lura* wants you to make up your mind."

"Do you want him or not?" Sarah asked, as if to confirm the rabbit's statement. "I can't keep my co-worker waiting forever."

"Yeah, I'll buy him. How much are you asking?"

"Are you kidding? There's no charge — I want him out of here. But for thirty bucks, I'll throw in the cage."

Simon looked the Mini Rex over. Should he buy it with the cage or take it as it was? Clara's picture came to mind, of this very same rabbit with a pair of fangs. The recollection helped him decide.

"I'll take the cage," he said, stifling a shiver.

The walk from the pet store was far from easy. It wasn't the distance — a mere six blocks — it wasn't the cage either, although it was awkward to carry. The hard part was the passenger. The rabbit — he claimed his name was Cletho — kept yelling how it wanted out and was sick and tired of being pushed around. And whenever Simon stumbled slightly, the rabbit would insult him, calling him clumsy, dumb, a *lura*-lover.

"What's a *lura*-lover?"

"As if you don't know."

"I don't."

"Let me free and maybe I'll tell you."

"You'll run away and my questions won't get answered."

"If you don't free me, I'll rip your lungs out! *Lura*-lover! *Lura*-lover!"

41

They were walking by Henry. The bum was drunk as usual, but Simon was sure the shouting would wake him. There were also neighbours milling about and he was certain they would look his way to find out who was making this ruckus. But again no one noticed the screaming.

"You're wasting your breath," Simon said. "These people can't hear you."

"Of course dey can't hear me. But you can, *lura*-lover."

"I wish I couldn't. But listen, we're almost home. If you behave yourself, we'll talk a little, I'll let you go, and you can do what you want. Okay?"

"Okay, *lura*-lover."

"And don't call me that. It's really annoying."

"Course it's annoyin'. Dat's why I'm sayin' it."

Simon climbed the front porch. Setting Cletho down, he opened the door and scanned the hallway to check that the coast was clear. Emma was banging pots in the kitchen, Ian (he knew) was over at a friend's, and his parents hadn't returned from work yet. Supper was scheduled for 7:15, giving him time to interrogate Cletho.

It took him sixty seconds to retrieve the cage, run upstairs, and duck into his room. Once inside, he turned the key in the lock.

"Okay," he said, eyeing his "guest," "I want answers."

"I have questions too," Cletho sneered. Its eyes were on Simon's and the effect was unsettling. "Who are you 'xactly? What tribe are you from?"

"Tribe? I have no tribe. My name is Simon and …"

"Can it, sonny. I want de truth."

"That is the truth. Look, just answer my questions and don't spin me in circles! I'm the human and you're the rabbit!"

Cletho narrowed his eyes at Simon. If the scene hadn't been so crazy, Simon would have laughed. A rabbit was eyeing him like a cop sizing up a possible suspect. Finally it nodded, understanding it was stuck unless it clued Simon in.

"Let's get one thing straight," it growled, "I ain't no rabbit. I'm a *kaba*, a soul. I needed a *vadh* or vessel to hide in. I was losin' steam 'cause I was floatin' too long. So I finds dis rabbit 'n I takes it over, not knowin' de owner would stick it in a cage 'n haul it to a pet shop in the city."

"Hang on." Simon was frowning. "Are you saying you're not part of this rabbit? Instead you're what, a soul of some kind?"

"Dat's what I'm sayin'. I'm a kaba, or spirit, dat can project all over. Transmigration, you *luras* call it. Only I need a *vadh* or body to rest in."

"Do you always hide in rabbits?"

"Any vadh'll do, dogs, elephants, birds, gerbils. So long as de vadh's larger dan a mouse. If it's any smaller, I can't squeeze in. Our leader can, but he's a *Khalkon*."

"You have a leader? You're not alone?"

"I belong to dis group dat calls demselves *bolkhs*. Dey're all kabas 'n deys number in de t'ousands."

Simon shook his head in disbelief. Having a rabbit talk was crazy enough, but the situation was getting odder by the minute. A spirit was comforting him. A spirit! And he's called himself what? A *bolkh* or something? And how was a spirit able to address him?

"How can you talk to me in spirit form?"

"Dat's de question, ain't it, bud? *Bolkhs* 'n *luras* don't never talk togedder."

"You keep saying that word, *luras*."

"Dat's what we bolkhs call human beins. Like I was sayin', we don't talk to luras, 'n dat must mean you ain't no human neither. Your vadh may be human, but your kaba ain't. How else could you get *bolkhin* — dat's our native tongue."

"You're not speaking English?"

"Course I ain't. 'N no one can hear bolkhin 'less he understands it."

 Simon shook his head. This story was rolling out of control. Luras, kabas, bolkhs, and vadhs. How was he involved in this nonsense?

"Where do I come in?" he asked.

"Dat's what I'm wonderin'," Cletho answered, "You ain't no *vrindh* …"

"A *vrindh*?"

"Dat's someone who's a mix of bolkh 'n lura. Dey's has special properties but deir kabas can't project. If you can hear me, you ain't one of dem. 'N you ain't no *limnl* neither."

"A *limnl*? What's that?"

"A limnl's a bolkh dat's been fused wid a *shatl*."

"That's very helpful," Simon said impatiently. "What's a *shatl*?"

"Geez, you sure are ignorant! Okay, you've got vadhs, right? Dose are bodies dat bolkhs can hide in, like dis rabbit fer instance? So a shatl's a human vadh. You got dat straight?"

"I guess."

"Okay. De problem wid shatls is dat kabas can't grab 'em de way we can a dog or rabbit. Lura kabas are too strong to displace, unless deys is *lakhn*, broken dat is."

"Broken?"

"Drunk or loony or unconscious or drugged. Dose luras we can climb inside. 'N we call dese occupied luras *hemindhs*. De problem wid *hemindhs*, t'ough, is dat de occupancy don't last long. When a drunk gets sober, de bolkh is expelled. Right?"

"If you say so." Simon was remembering the night before, when for an instant he'd seen the world through Henry's eyes, as the bum had been lying there drunk as a skunk. And earlier, when he'd guessed that Winston's mom was sick? Was that because of the Ritalin in Winston? Were he and Henry — what had Cletho called it — *lakhn*?

"But dere's a way to sink in permanently. I'm talkin' about newborns. For de first hour after birth, de lura soul can be taken over. Forever, dat is. If you're a bolkh 'n be lucky to find a baby lura, den you can kick him out 'n make his shatl yours. Dis bolkh is called a limnl, see? De problem is it don't happen a lot."

"Look," Simon said, trying to control his irritation, "you still haven't told me where I fit in."

"Yeah, well, you ain't a lura, nor a hemindh, nor a limnl, nor a vrindh."

"Instead of saying what I'm not, how about saying what I am?"

"Dat's my point! I've exhausted all de assortments! De only udder one is outta de question. I'm talkin' 'bout a *woplh*."

Simon's eyes lit up. A *woplh*? That was strange. It was the word Clara had mentioned earlier. In fact, it was the only word he'd ever heard her speak. He looked at Cletho, who was eyeing him sharply.

"Youse know somet'in', bud? I gets de ideer you've heard dis word before."

"You're right," Simon confessed. "Someone mentioned it this afternoon. I've never heard it used before, then it's spoken twice the very same day. What are the chances?"

"Who mentioned it, bud?" Cletho asked. He was staring hard at Simon now, as if trying hard to see inside him. He was straining against the lid with his paws and the plastic almost snapped beneath this pressure. "Who said it, bud?" he asked again, his black eyes burning.

"Some girl I know," Simon answered. Cletho's intensity had him nervous. "She's our nanny's daughter. She's autistic and can barely speak."

"You don't say," Cletho said with a chuckle. "How very interestin'."

"So what's a woplh?" Simon asked, still not satisfied with Cletho's explanation, "And why did that girl mention it today, and ..."

But Cletho wouldn't cooperate further. He was no longer eyeing Simon but pounding the lid with his head and paws, like a convict trying to break out of jail.

"I ain't answerin' no more questions! Not 'less you free me!"

"If you're a kaba, why not break out on your own?"

"'Cause my kaba's too big to squeeze t'rough de mesh! And when I'm out, whatta I do? I need a vadh to hide in. But open up if you want your questions answered! 'N believe me, brudder, dere's stuff you gotta know!"

This said, it buried its head in its paws. While the Mini Rex looked cute and endearing, it was clear Cletho was suffering badly. It was also clear he wouldn't speak any further unless he was given his freedom. Truthfully, Simon didn't like the idea. While the rabbit was harmless, the bolkh seemed far from stable.

But he did have crucial information to share. His description of luras, bolkhs, and vrindhs was most intriguing, to say the least, and Simon wanted to hear a lot more. That meant taking a chance with Cletho.

Without a word he unlatched four clips, lifted the lid, and put it aside. An instant later Cletho was out and running. For the next few minutes he hopped and jumped, full of joy to be stretching his muscles.

"All right," Simon said, when Cletho came to a stop, "let's return to my questions."

"Look," Cletho said, hopping close to Simon, "we could talk for hours but it wouldn't get us nowhere. If you wanna know who you are, and what we bolkhs are 'bout, de best solution is to transmigrate."

"That's crazy. I'm not able to."

"You can. Definitely. Like it or not, you're some kinda

bolkh and dat means you can project for sure. Open de window and give it a try."

"Open the window?"

"There ain't no projectin' through solid objects. Go on. Open it. You'll be thankin' me soon."

Cletho was pushing Simon with his snout, to encourage him to give projection a try. Laughing nervously and shaking his head, Simon stood and opened the window. For good measure, he unlatched the snaps on the screen and shoved its meshing out of the way. His window faced the street and he studied the scene. His parents' cars were in the driveway — he'd been so engrossed with Cletho that he hadn't heard them come in. The Gleason kids were playing in the street, Jimmy Fields was lifting weights in his room, and Henry was sprawled out down below, "soused to the gills," as his mother would say.

"Empty your mind and think 'bout nothin'. Pretend you're a wave on de sea."

"That's thinking about something."

"Shh. Not a word. Just look outside at de fallin' darkness and imagine you are part of de scene. Concentrate. Let your body melt away. First your fingers, den your toes, den your legs …"

"This isn't working."

"No talkin'! Your body ain't yours. So find what's yours. De shape inside dat never changes. Go on, search it out. Yeah, you're relaxin.'"

Simon was about to say this was crazy when, for the tiniest instant, something … slipped. His legs seemed to collapse beneath him, like a tree's roots somehow coming undone. Then they were back in place and propping him up.

"Good. You're almost dere," Cletho crooned. "Keep gazin' at de sky. You belong dere as much as you belong in dis shell."

Simon squinted at the trees outside and, beyond their branches, at the pitch-black heavens. The clouds were heavy with impending rain and two birds were visible — they were flying west. He yearned to join them. His legs, his arms, they felt tingly and light, as if they were made of helium and could float right off.

Wait, they weren't floating! *He* was floating! He could see his hands below. They were resting on the windowsill, together with the rest of his frame. He was like a fly on the ceiling looking down at the room and …

"You're almost dere," Cletho spoke from far away, from the far side of the earth, in fact. "Go for it. Leave everythin' except de part dat's you. Go, go, go!"

These words ignited him. Without having time to think about his actions, Simon felt a final obstacle slip off, as if his core was breaking free of an anchor. There was a sound of something tearing, he thought, and a feeling of lightness and absolute freedom. His senses were melting and in place of them were electrical pulses, sharp and clean and beautifully precise. He could hear and see even better this way. In fact, he'd never felt so real before, so pure, so true, so … uncorrupted.

He was floating upward. His house was growing smaller, the street as well — the Gleason kids were still running about. He was higher than the tallest tree and had a breathtaking view. Queen Elizabeth Park was below, then the Conservatory, the Botanical Gardens, and, over to the north, the buildings downtown. And still he kept rising. The harbour appeared, English Bay, Burrard Inlet, and, way in the distance, the Fraser River.

He was amazed beyond words and tempted to climb higher. Maybe he could reach outer space and get a glimpse of North America. While the thought sent a spasm through him, a voice urged caution. The sky was empty and, as he considered its depths, he felt a pang of isolation. This beauty, this remoteness, was too inhuman. He had to get back, to his body, his family, his room's four walls.

No sooner did he think about home than his kaba started its descent to earth. As fast as an eagle, he plummeted downward. His neighbourhood drew closer, the park, the trees, his street …

There. He was beside his house. Relief flooded him, pride as well. He'd done it. He'd done something amazing. Over a space of ten seconds he'd climbed a dazzling height. He couldn't wait to tell his family. He would do so as soon as he'd "docked" with his body, which he could see five metres away in the distance. It was standing at the window, like a mannequin in a store, with its big bones, slick brown hair, and a blank, goofy kind of expression.

But wait. His body… it was grinning, not a kind smile but a nasty, two-faced one. And… hey! His hands were gripping the rabbit which…. No! With a vicious twist, they snapped the animal's neck. With lightning speed they tossed the carcass out and closed the window with a heart-stopping bang.

Simon hit the pane. He screamed at Cletho to get out of his body, to abandon it at once or else!

His voice was a squeak and Cletho paid no attention. He was busy admiring his shatl in a mirror, like someone studying a new set of clothes.

As he floated about in the dark outside, Simon realized he had absolutely nowhere to go.

Chapter Five

For two long minutes Simon couldn't move. Was it possible? Had he really been expelled from his body? His arms, legs, heart and lungs, these were no longer his to control? He pressed up against the window and stared into his room. Cletho was still in front of the mirror, primping and preening, and testing things out. Simon felt a pang of despair. He'd been robbed of his most personal belonging and there was nothing he could do about it.

Adding insult to injury, thunder sounded in the distance.

Cletho moved away from the mirror. Glancing at the window he waved to Simon, then exited the room and passed downstairs. His dinner was ready, Simon thought, and this thief was going to take his seat at the table. His mom would kiss him and his dad would muss his hair, little guessing they were dealing with a stranger.

Simon started panicking. What were Cletho's plans? Did he mean to harm his family? Was he intending to set the house on fire or poison their food or attack while they were sleeping? Hadn't he threatened to cut Simon's throat? And if he could steal a body, he was capable of murder.

As Simon's worries mounted, he started feeling — thin. Something inside him was coming undone, as if he was a coat or shirt and the threads were coming loose. He was losing focus and felt cold all over, as if some inner spark were dying. His house, the trees, the lawn, the street, everything was fading — no, *he* was fading. Within moments there'd be nothing left and the soul of Simon Carpenter would be no more.

Dimly he recalled Cletho's words, that he'd lost steam from floating outside too long. The same was happening to Simon now and the only way to keep himself from dying was to find a vadh and slip inside it. But where and who and how exactly?

He glanced around frantically. On their eavestrough a sparrow was roosting. He zoomed toward it but the bird took wing. Darn! In a sweat he was thinking about that rogue raccoon, the one that was always rooting through their garbage. It had to be lurking somewhere. He floated to the oak on their lawn and scanned its trunk and branches. Nothing.

The cold intensified. He was getting desperate. Looking round everywhere, he settled his gaze (whatever that meant) on a great big mound lying at the start of the alley. Henry. The bum was sprawled out in his makeshift shelter, drunk as always and snoring loudly. Simon swiftly drifted close, until he was positioned directly above him. For an instant he studied Henry's beard, long greasy hair, and unwashed figure. His belly was visible and his mouth was open. Simon had never seen teeth so brown before.

Now what?

How did it work? How did a spirit enter a body? Was he supposed to go in through the mouth or nostrils, like a spelunker jumping into a cave? And where was he supposed to settle? In the brain, kidney, lungs, liver? And if he did wind up in the right location, what would he do next? How did a kaba assume control? It wasn't as if Henry came with pedals and a steering wheel. He shivered as another wave of cold coursed through him. Desperate to do something, he leapt forward.

How weird. It was like diving into a sponge of energy and Jell-O. A stickiness encompassed him and he felt a thousand shocks at once. He was also being stretched and stretched, while an impossible weight bore down on him, as if a dozen grand pianos were being stacked on his shoulders. And his manner of sensing things was altered. The impressions were richer but not as sharply defined.

Then everything gelled and he felt human again: he was seeing through a pair of eyes, sensing sour tastes, and feeling cold on his belly. He moved to tuck his shirt in and push some hair from his eyes.

Wait a moment — Simon almost screamed. Whom did the belly and hair belong to? With a thrill of shock he felt himself over. Geez! He'd done it! He'd actually done it! He'd burrowed inside Henry and taken him over.

He stood, very shakily. While Henry's limbs responded to his thoughts, they didn't feel like they were a hundred percent his. Each seemed heavy, wooden, and unpredictable, as if his arms and legs were prosthetics maybe. That explained why he was wobbling and trying desperately to balance. It didn't help either that his veins were full of booze.

No. That wasn't true. It was a blessing the body was all boozed up. Lurking in its depths was someone else. This presence was dormant, unconscious even, but Simon could sense it still — like when you walk into a darkened room and know that someone, or something, is hiding in the shadows. This kaba belonged to Henry, of course. In the outside world the bum was often irritable, so what would his reaction be when he discovered Simon in his pilot's seat?

As Simon mulled this question over, there was a crack of thunder. He directed his gaze toward the Carpenter house. His family. Cletho. How could he forget? That thief was at the dinner table and poised to strike at any moment. Maybe he was stabbing them as Simon stood there gawking. He had to act. Focusing his thoughts, he piloted Henry across the lawn.

It must have looked hilarious. He was moving like a baby learning to walk. Three times he stumbled and struck the ground. His clumsiness would have made a zombie look like Fred Astaire. Still, the stakes were high and he persevered. After a few minutes, and a few more falls, he was poised outside the window that looked into their dining room.

He'd been expecting something awful — Cletho with a knife in hand and blood streaming everywhere. In some ways it was worse. Everyone was eating and having a great time. Cletho was sitting in Simon's chair, devouring his food, and talking up a storm. His dad and Ian were laughing at his joke, while his mom was smiling and sipping wine, a sign she was in excellent spirits. Emma was relaxed and chuckling too.

Simon felt sick. Instead of fearing Cletho, his family adored him. In fact, they were acting as if they preferred his company to Simon's. Cletho, too, seemed happy. Far from threatening the Carpenter family, he was doing his best to make a good impression, as if he were glad to be part of a family now. Simon should have been hugely relieved — after all, his loved ones weren't in any danger. But it ate at him that Cletho felt so much at home, and that his parents couldn't tell this creep was an imposter.

There was another clap of thunder and his mom suddenly spied him. Her smile died. She spilled her wine and pointed nervously toward the window. Everyone looked in Simon's direction, fearfully and mouths half-open in shock. Cletho alone was amused. He knew that Simon was taking shelter in Henry. Itching to confront the thief, Simon left the window and lumbered toward the front door.

He was approaching it when his dad stepped out. Ian and Cletho were right behind, followed by Emma, and then his mom. Emma was carrying a plate with food.

"Good evening Henry," his father said. "You seem a little bothered this evening."

Simon tried to speak but nothing would come. While he could move Henry's tongue a little, it had the flexibility of a two-by-four.

"In case you're hungry," his dad went on, "we've brought you out some dinner. Emma's chili is out of this world and her cornbread's the best I've ever tasted."

Emma offered him a plate of chili with bread on the side. Simon didn't take the food but struggled to speak. A clap of thunder accompanied his gurgles.

"He's drunk," Cletho jeered. How strange. Instead of his usual tough-sounding accent, he sounded exactly like Simon now.

"What else is new?" Ian said. "Have you ever seen him sober?"

"They ought to lock him up," Cletho snarled, "and toss away the key."

"Simon!" his mother barked. "What a rude thing to say!"

"You shouldn't insult someone when he's down," Emma spoke. "Henry!" she cried, grasping Simon's hand. "Take this food. If you're still feeling poorly, let us know and we'll fetch help."

"What he needs is a bath," Cletho jeered. "He smells like a sewer."

"Simon!" Mrs. Carpenter snapped. "What's got into you? Enough of that!"

"Shh!" his dad cried. "He's trying to speak."

Sure enough, by concentrating hard, Simon was flexing his tongue more freely. The problem was he couldn't bend it enough and the words that emerged were barely coherent. When he said, "I'm your real son," it came out mangled.

"He says he has a gun!" Cletho warned.

"I think he mentioned rum," Ian said.

"In that case," his father said, "you should eat before you start drinking rum."

Simon tried again. This time he attempted to say, "I am Simon."

"He told us to die," Cletho cried. "Talk about nerve!"

"No, he said *he's* dying," Ian said. "What's the matter? You're not feeling well?"

Shaking with frustration, Simon decided his best bet was to write something down. That's why he reached toward his father. Like every engineer, his dad had several pens in his breast pocket. Simon intended to take one of these and scrawl a message on his palm. Unfortunately he gauged the distance wrong: instead of taking a pen, he grabbed his dad's shirt. A clap of thunder intensified his gesture.

"Go easy!" Mr. Carpenter warned.

"Henry!" Ian yelled. "Let go of my dad!"

"He's going for your throat!" Cletho screamed. "He means to hurt you!"

Emma sprang forward. Never one to shrink in the face of a threat, she flew at Simon and chopped his arm. Instantly he released his dad and staggered back a couple of paces. Yelling at everyone to run inside, she stood between Simon and the rest of the gang, prepared to hit him if he made a move. Moments later his dad called to her, urging her to run inside

58

too. Edging back, she retreated to the porch, climbed the steps, and ducked inside. Simon managed to yell "Emma!" clearly, but the door closed noisily and drowned him out.

He saw them through a window. His dad was shaking his head in relief, convinced they'd had a narrow escape. Ian was jumping up and down, Cletho was mouthing a string of insults, while Emma was brandishing a candlestick, just in case "Henry" tried to force his way in. And his mom? She was calling the police.

Simon stayed on the porch. He had no choice. If he was going to get his shatl back, he couldn't walk away. He called out Emma's name again and added he was Simon, the real Simon Carpenter. A clap of thunder drowned him out, while Cletho was making a commotion inside to prevent the family from hearing him, the jerk. "I'll just keep at it," Simon was thinking, except that another sound intruded.

Sirens. The cops were coming. They were two blocks off but closing in quickly.

Simon cursed. If the cops got hold of him, they would haul him off and his parents wouldn't learn how matters really stood. He couldn't be arrested. To the accompaniment of yet more thunder, he fled the porch and dragged Henry across the lawn, like a porter handling a weight of heavy baggage. The sirens were close. To make matters worse the rain was starting.

What should he do? If he stayed on the street, the cops would nab him. The only other choice was the neighbourhood alley, never mind it was overgrown and muddy and full of bugs and spiders. Gathering his rags, he plunged straight in.

The weeds and ferns and undergrowth received him. A patch of mud swiftly brought him to his knees. As he swore, the police pulled up: the flashers from their cars drowned the alley in blood. Doors flew open and beams of light probed everywhere. Cletho was yelling that the bum was heading west.

Simon crawled frantically. Rain was streaming down his face, his shoes were sodden and his pants were caked with mud. His heart was hammering and, ouch, a shard of glass dug into his palm. And he didn't even know where he was headed, did he?

As bad as things were, they suddenly got worse.

"Who the hell are you?" someone growled straight at him.

Chapter Six

"**Y**ou deaf or somethin'? What are you doin' inside me, pal?"

Simon shivered violently. Henry's kaba was stirring. The effects of the booze were wearing thin and the bum was regaining control of himself. He was confused to find Simon inside him and his confusion would turn to rage soon enough.

"Answer me! Who are you and why are you inside me? This is my space in case you ain't noticed! And why are we on all fours in this here alley when it's spittin' cats 'n dogs outside?"

Simon was thinking hard. The alley ran on for five hundred metres and ended in a street that the cops would be watching. Halfway down was an unpaved path that connected the alley to the local park. This park was huge, had lots of places to hide in, and led to a dozen neighbouring streets. If he reached this park, he could evade the police. But they would have to move like crazy.

"Hey pal! Slow down! I'm an old fogey and ain't used to athletics!"

Simon felt repelled. Henry's presence was rubbing against him, as if they were stuck in a matchbox together. He could practically taste the bum's emotions, as well as his sweat and rancid breath. His sodden beard was scratchy and could do with a washing.

"Who are you to complain 'bout my hygiene, eh? It ain't as if I invited you in. And why the heck is my right hand bleedin'?"

Simon realized he had to check his thoughts, otherwise Henry would be able to read them. He was about to apologize when a light stabbed near them. He threw Henry's bulk to the ground. That's when Henry started to gurgle. He understood his limbs lay outside his control and the realization had him panic-stricken. In his fear he wanted to cry for help. Simon had to stop him. By sheer force of will, he "squeezed" the bum's kaba — it was as if they were speeding in a car on the highway and wrestling each other for control of the wheel. Simon was able to take it in hand but knew that Henry would soon be stronger than him. What had Cletho said? "Occupancy don't last long. When a drunk gets sober, de bolkh is expelled."

He had to act fast.

"Listen," Simon said, *"I'll explain things later. Right now we have to escape the police."*

"The fuzz?" Henry squawked. *"What do they want? I ain't done nothin' 'cept loiter a bit."*

"They think you attacked the Carpenter family. If they nab us, they'll throw you in jail for sure."

"Jail? Lordy. I can't be nabbed. There ain't no beer nor whisky in jail."

"Then stop calling for help and let's work together."

"Okey doke. But promise me this: you ain't a ghost or demon, right?"

Before Simon could answer there were shouts from behind. Two cops were in the alley and closing in fast. Anxious to evade them now, Henry stopped fighting and handed the "wheel" to Simon, who manoeuvred them forward, past brambles, ferns, puddles, and garbage. The rain was driving into his face. Where was that path? It couldn't be far.

"You see that fence?" Henry spoke up, reading his thoughts. He was "pointing" left to a chain-link fence.

"Yeah."

"The path is behind it. The government erected the fence 'cause lotsa houses were bein' burgled."

Simon glanced around. The bobbing light beams were getting close and the cops were maybe a minute behind.

"Let's climb it."

"No way. It must be seven feet and I ain't no pole vaulter."

"Hang on tight."

Simon focused especially hard. Bending the bum's legs and tensing his muscles, he allowed the strength inside them to gather. When the sinew was shaking with the pent-up force, Simon released it all at once. Henry would have screamed had Simon let him. His shatl left the ground like a rocket, arched eight feet, and cleared the fence. A moment later it landed in some bushes, just as Simon intended. Apart from some bruises, Henry would be fine.

"You maniac!" Henry fumed. *"You could've killed me!"*

As the old man cursed, Simon hurried them on. The path was maybe three feet wide and lined with fences on either side, behind which were houses and well-trimmed lawns. Simon pictured people going about their business, doing homework, cleaning dishes, watching TV together, dry and warm and safe from the dark. Would he ever enjoy these routines again? What insanity had caused him to buy that rabbit?

The sound of panting distracted him. A large wooden fence stood to their right. Behind it was a tiny yard patrolled by a dog, a hulking German shepherd. The brute was standing near the fence, its collar clinking and a growl in its throat. It was about to bark and betray their location.

"Lordy," Henry whimpered. *"That's one big dog."*

Simon spied it between two planks. Without hesitation he jumped from Henry to the dog. He sank into it instantly — its vadh was simple compared to Henry's shatl — and yelled *"Quiet!"* to its startled soul. He added, *"Good boy!"* when the kaba complied, then drifted back to Henry again. This took a second and the results were telling. The dog retreated and troubled them no longer.

"You frighten me," Henry said. *"I mean, the way you gave the bejesus to that mutt. You must be an evil spirit or somethin'."*

"Maybe I'm a good one?"

"I doubt that. A good one wouldn't waste his time on me. I want you out."

"Soon. We're almost there."

They were in the park. Night had fallen on its sprawling grounds. The odd lamppost beat the shadows back, but the rain and darkness had the upper hand. The place was too large for the cops to search thoroughly. If they laid low …

"I ain't lingerin' here, if that's what you're thinkin'."

"If we leave right now, they'll catch us for sure. The cops will be watching the nearby streets."

"There are too many exits and they ain't watchin' 'em all."

Simon paused. He could see the guy was getting stronger with each minute. Angrier too. If he chased Simon out, Cletho would triumph. So how could he evade the cops and at the same time maintain his perch in Henry?

Behind them he heard barking. The cops had climbed the fence and were creeping by the German shepherd. Any minute now …

"The fuzz is comin'. So what's it to be?"

"Hang on a sec. Let me scout things out."

Gathering himself, Simon shot into the air — his sudden weightlessness was thrilling. Climbing thirty metres, he scanned the region. Besides the park's unending hollows he could see the path and the approaching police, as well as the streets where their partners lay waiting — they were parked on Dinmont, Midlothian, and Ontario. Just east of them was Main Street, brightly lit and packed with people. He could just make out a fancy boutique, an antiques shop, a liquor store …

A liquor store.

He flitted back to Henry. Re-entering the guy was like digging through sand. And regaining control required more of an effort, as the effects of the booze were fast receding. He had to get him drunk and quickly. That's why he steered them to Peveril Avenue. From there they'd hoof it to East 28th and Main.

"So what's our destination, ghost?"

"Don't worry. You won't be disappointed."

"Okay, buster. I've had 'nuff of this crap."

They were on East 28th, a block away from Main. Henry was antsy now and squeezing Simon hard. It was getting hard to force the bum to walk in one direction. Every few steps the shatl would stop and Simon would have to wrestle to keep it moving. Even so a leg was dragging and Henry's arm kept punching out — he'd wrested back control of this limb. They must have been a funny sight. Some pedestrians couldn't help but smile when they saw a bum wrestling with his inner demons.

"You hear me? You gotta go!"

"You've been patient, Henry …"

"You darn tootin' I've been patient …"

"And I'd like to show my appreciation."

"Yeah? How? You ain't got nothin', not a body even."

"Well, how about a drink?"

"I oughta punch you for hoistin' my rear in the air."

"Sure. Fine. But how about a drink?"

"What's that you said? Is someone servin' drinks?"

"You bet. Take a look over there."

Simon pointed to the liquor store across the road. His plan was simple. He would get Henry stewed, put his kaba to sleep, then steer him back to the house where he'd somehow take his body back from Cletho. It wasn't nice to play on Henry's weakness, but Simon couldn't think of a better idea. Not if he was going to get his old life back.

"You shoulda told me earlier. If I'da known you wanted to get me a drink, I wouldn't have been a stick in the mud, even though you ain't got business here. So what are we waitin' for? Santa Claus or somethin'?"

Far from fighting Simon, Henry helped him walk his shatl across the road. The force of his desire to drink was shocking. If Henry was in any way possessed, the demon was his alcoholism and not Simon's presence.

A minute later they were wandering the store and examining the bottles of booze on display. Henry was salivating and smacking his lips. He was like a kid in a candy shop, only this brand of candy was like TNT. Still, the booze would prove most useful to Simon; that was why he urged Henry to choose his poison.

"I'm fond of Jack and John," Henry joked. *"Mind if I take both?"*

"Who are Jack and John?"

"Jack Daniels and Johnny Walker. You ain't a drinker, are you?"

"I'm sixteen years old."

"That so? You seem older than that. I mean, you smell real old, ancient like. But old, young, what do I care? The point is how we goin' to pay for my 'buddies'? They're real good friends but they don't come cheap."

"Leave it to me. Grab hold of the bottles and await my signal."

Simon abandoned Henry and wafted to the back of the store, the part reserved for employees only. Ignoring the many cases of booze, he moved into an alcove that was furnished with a table and three chairs. There was a crack in the wall, which he navigated easily. After searching a minute, he found what he was after — a mouse.

It was nibbling a sandwich that a worker had discarded. When Simon swooped inside it, its kaba was so tiny and frail that it moved aside and let him take things over. Simon laughed as he directed the paws and they responded instantly. But his eyesight was weird. He could discern every object around him but things were blurry, even the stuff nearby. And the colours weren't normal. He could see blues and greens but the reds were funny.

He was wasting time. Without further ado, he steered the mouse outside the wall, across the storage room, and into the store. Spying people in the central aisle, he moved into an empty one — it was lined with bottles of wine from Australia. To lessen the chance of being spotted he ran along the join between the shelves and floor, beneath an inch-long overhang of wood. Unlike Henry's shatl, which was slow and clumsy, the mouse was fast and easily steered. It was like driving a souped-up car.

He neared a counter with a cash register. The wooden structure was like the Rocky Mountains, the way it rose ninety degrees and towered above him. Its sanded grain contained many abrasions and, leaping upward, Simon grabbed them with his claws. He almost whooped.

Mounting this structure was as easy as climbing stairs. In the blink of an eye he'd managed to clear the top.

The cashier was reading *The Exorcist*. He would look up every couple of seconds to ensure his customers weren't up to no good. In particular, he was keeping an eye on Henry, whose clothes didn't bring the word "respectable" to mind.

Amazed the cashier hadn't noticed him yet — he was standing on the countertop — Simon ran at his book. The guy noticed now. With a shriek, he tossed the book in the air. Landing on the counter, Simon scurried to its edge and scrambled down to the tiled floor. Once the mouse was headed to the back, Simon left its vadh and returned to Henry.

"Hijacking" Henry was far from easy. He was one-fifth drunk and four-fifths concrete — or so it seemed. Simon did finally manage to worm his way inside and swiftly directed the shatl past the exit, with "Jack" and "John" in Henry's hands and two more bottles in his coat's side pockets. The cashier didn't see. His eyes were watching the mouse in aisle four and everyone else was transfixed too.

"This calls for a party," Henry cried, clinking his bottles together.

"But not here," Simon warned, worried the cops might spot them.

"Not here," Henry agreed. *"I have a different spot in mind."*

Chapter Seven

"Hey, Henry! You ain't said who you prefer. John or Jack?"

"I don't choose between friends. Jack has a woody taste that gets the furnace goin'. John is more like smoke than wood and tastes like courage in the thick of battle. Neither gent will let you down."

"De guy's a philosopher! Someone get Socrates here a lengtha sausage!"

Simon was antsy. It had been hours since their trip to the liquor store. He'd assumed that Henry would drink himself stupid and allow him to take his shatl over. With that in hand, he would have made his way home and somehow driven Cletho from his body. But the bum had disappointed him. Taking tiny sips of Jack, he'd headed up to Terminal Avenue. When he'd reached the edge of a railroad yard, he'd entered it through a tear in a fence, wandered beneath a metal underpass, and wound up in a large, abandoned clearing. Junk was scattered everywhere: scrap metal, car seats, empty crates, and broken glass.

"Hey! Don't guzzle! This booze has gotta last 'til mornin' — by my est'mit that means 'nudder two hours."

"Pass th' Jack, willya. My pa's name was Jack. Now dere's a man who could hold his likker. De demon spirit, my ma used to call it and, shur 'nuff, when he'd filled hisself, it was like a forin' presence was eruptin' inside him."

"You bringin' that old subject up 'gain?"

"Jimmy's right. Every time we gather, it's always the same. Once the booze starts settlin', we talk 'bout the drunks wid ghosts inside 'em."

Henry had travelled here to meet his "colleagues" — that's how he'd described them, at least. This group consisted of men like Henry, grizzled boozers with no place to go and whose life ambition was to drink themselves sick. But they could be generous. Take Henry, for example. With four quality bottles in hand, his immediate instinct was to find his pals so that he could share this windfall with them.

Eight "colleagues" had assembled and greeted Henry like a hero. They'd started a fire, arranged seats around the flames, and got a mess of sausages frying, as well as potatoes and sliced up onions. In addition to Henry's John and Jack, there was wine, gin, and a quantity of beer. For hours the group had been drinking and talking. While the booze was definitely kicking in — two bums were slumped against each other — Henry wasn't so far gone that Simon could nab him.

"Those stories are true," Henry ventured. "I can say so from 'xper'yens. Just today a spook grabbed me and took hold of my limbs."

"Is that you talkin' or your best friend Jack…?"

"Easy there," Simon whispered to the bum. *"Some things are better left unspoken."*

"It ain't either my friend Jack! And how d'you s'pose I got my hands on four bottles?"

"I figured you cashed in some of yer stocks," a guy named Jimmy joked.

As the bums laughed uproariously and passed the bottles again, Simon twisted with impatience. His family would be gone from the house by eight. If he didn't catch them, he would have to wait until nightfall, at which point Henry would be sober again. He could confront Cletho over at the school, assuming the bolkh would be attending classes, only the staff would never let him into the building, not if he were travelling in the likes of Henry. The long and short of it was he had to get moving.

"Hey, Sam!" Jimmy cried. "I see yer knockin' off togedder wid Gilles."

"Yeah, I'm knackered. And Gilles can't keep his eyelids open."

"Take anudder swallow. Dat'll keep you goin'. 'N pour a drop o' Jack into Gilles. It ain't civilized to sit wid us 'n not be drinkin'."

"You got dat right," Gilles mumbled, taking another swallow of booze.

Simon eyed this pair. It occurred to him that Henry wasn't the only "ride" there. Any drunk would do, once the liquor stormed his senses. And to judge by Sam's state, or better yet Gilles', a ride would be available soon.

The bums kept partying, only their talk grew sombre. They discussed old pals who'd vanished over the years. Some had died while riding the rails, others because the cold had claimed them, and others because they'd taken one too many beatings. Then Jimmy described a colleague named Angus. A few months back, in the Seattle region, Angus had stolen a truck and crashed into a train, derailing it and killing a dozen people. The FBI said it was the work of extremists, but Jimmy knew the real cause: booze turned bad.

Other tales followed, of bums who'd acted just as strangely, across the entire continent, the Yukon included.

"It's those demons," Henry said. "They take hold of us boozers. Unless they come ready packed in the bottle."

"I don't believe in spooks," Jimmy said. "Just the grain that goes into a whisky's makin'."

"There are demons all right," a guy named Ivan broke in. "I don't get drunk easy, in case you ain't noticed, but the folks who do open themselves to spooks."

"Like this evenin'," Henry said. "You wouldn't believe how high I jumped 'cuz a spook zapped me from deep inside. Eight feet it must've been."

Again Simon was going to warn Henry, only he noticed something odd going on. There was a tiny movement around Sam and Gilles. Something at their feet was twitching slightly. Simon flinched. It was a rat, a huge one. The odd thing was it was ignoring the food. Gilles was so dopy that a length of sausage had escaped his fingers. Normally a rat would have killed for such food, but not this specimen. It was ... distracted.

Simon felt chilled. What was going on?

"No way you jumped eight feet," Jimmy jeered. "Who d'you think you are? Superman or somethin'? You don't wear tights, for cryin' out loud."

"I believe him," Ivan spoke. "You know that fat ass Seymour? One time when he was floatin' on Scotch I seen him climb a buildin' like that hero Spiderman …"

The rat was still ignoring the sausage. Simon wanted to find out why. That's why he drifted off from Henry and wafted cautiously in the rat's direction. He could have rushed it but something told him to be careful.

"That spook I mentioned," Henry said, "he's on the prowl."

"Shut up about spooks," Jimmy growled. "Let's change the talk already."

Simon was hovering near the rat — he could see a couple of fleas in its fur. He approached the skull, admiring its orb-like eyes. Then he started. The rat and Gilles were whispering to each other — at least, there were bolkhs inside them who were having a chat. Despite his screaming nerves, he listened in.

"*Listen, Serdho,*" the rat was saying, "*this is really big news.*"

"*You don't think I've heard that one before, Pebhlo?*" Gilles replied.

"*This lead is strong,*" the rat insisted. "*A kaba was found this very evening. He was definitely bolkh but not vrindh or limnl. You know what that means?*"

"*You're saying he's a woplh!*" Serdho practically sneered. "*The one that gave Tarhlo the slip years ago?*"

"That's what I'm saying! And where there's a woplh, there's a hamax!"

"Yeah, well, who found this woplh?"

"Cletho — of the Khrastin tribe."

Again Simon started. Cletho? The same Cletho who'd robbed him some hours before? How had he managed…?

"… He was able to find Irdho who was riding a bird. He tells Irdho it's urgent and to pass the news quickly. Within hours it reaches Tarhlo and stirs his interest."

"I'll bet it does."

"He's so interested that he's making his way to Vancouver."

"Tarhlo's coming here?"

"That's what I'm saying. We're meeting at Koblansky's, at midnight tomorrow. It's the smell of blood, you know. Tarhlo loves it."

"He really thinks we've found a hamax?"

"He doesn't think. He knows. You'll be coming, I hope?"

"Are you kidding? If Tarhlo thinks it real, that's good enough for me."

Simon wanted to linger but his kaba was thinning. If he remained outside much longer, it wouldn't be good. That's why he moved off from the pair and plunged back into Henry. He sighed, glad to be inside again. But the question remained, who were these kabas and what did tomorrow's gathering mean?

"… I'm tellin' you," Jimmy said, "if we don't change this subject, I'm outta here."

"Speak to Gilles and that rat," Henry declared. "They can ver'fy what I'm sayin.'"

Nicholas Maes

"What are you talkin' 'bout?" Jimmy laughed.

"Don't do it!" Simon yelled to Henry, cursing himself for baring his thoughts so clearly. *"Those demons you're referring to are out to get us."*

"You mean, they're out to get you," Henry thought with a laugh. He cleared his throat and spoke aloud. Simon tried to stop him but he was too clear-minded to control. "That spook I mentioned? He said there's one inside in Gilles. 'N that rat beside him? It's got one too."

A hush seemed to fall on the group. It was followed by a laugh from Jimmy who was about to tell Henry he was full of crap. But Gilles beat him to it. Jumping to his feet, he stalked over to Henry. For a guy who was drunk, his movements were graceful.

"WHO ARE YOU? WHAT'S YOUR TRIBE? WHY ARE YOU HERE?"

The sound caused Simon to shake inside Henry. The vibrations hounded him and spun him in circles. The volume was so loud it seemed to swallow him whole.

"SPEAK UP! WHO ARE YOU? WHY DIDN'T YOU GREET US? I WANT AN ANSWER!"

As Simon bowed beneath this shock wave, he realized with a start that Henry didn't feel it. Serdho was speaking bolkhin and could be heard by Simon and no one else. From far away he heard Henry tell Gilles that he was crowding him in.

"LISTEN CLOSELY, BOLKH! ANSWER OUR QUESTIONS OR WE'LL HURT YOUR SHATL. WE'LL RIP HIM TO PIECES AND DRIVE YOU OUT!"

Without awaiting an answer, Gilles let Henry have it. Much to the old man's shock, he was punched in the face and knocked to the soil. As the others yelled and climbed to their feet, Gilles was preparing to hit Henry again. And the rat was scurrying forward, its yellow fangs bared.

"He's going to kill me!" Henry cried in fear. *"I can see it in his eyes!"*

"Don't worry. He's after me," Simon said. *"I'll quit your body and he'll leave you alone. Many thanks, Henry. You've been a great help."*

Simon leapt into the air. Henry screamed that the spook was gone and, sure enough, his attackers let him be. Moving off from the fire, they scanned the area around them.

"WHO ARE YOU?" Serdho yelled. *"DON'T THINK THAT YOU CAN HIDE! WE WILL FIND YOU AND WHEN WE DO ..."*

Simon had flown fifty metres or so. The vibrations were making him shiver and once again his kaba was starting to thin. He looked round frantically. Below him were some railroad ties, half overgrown with weeds, and in their midst a rat was skulking. Without hesitating, Simon swooped into this beast.

The rat posed no challenge; its kaba retreated and yielded its "controls." An instant later Simon was off and running. His goal was to escape these brutes and watch them from a distance. What had Cletho called an occupied body? Not *demins* or *hemans* ... *hemindhs*, that was it.

From behind he heard Jimmy yell, "Gilles! What's bugging you?"

Seconds later, Simon felt a hulking shape above him. Trusting his rat's instincts he skittered right — just in time: a boot came down and almost squashed him flat. He ducked into a line of bushes, glancing back quickly. While his rat's pupils made everything blurry, he could see that Gilles was closing in. And his pal Pebhlo was charging too.

Gilles' body landed mere inches from him, tossed like a rag doll by Serdho within. His hand tried grabbing Simon, who dodged it by entering a length of PVC tubing. Pebhlo followed in hot pursuit, gnashing at his hindparts to slow him down. Three times his fangs flashed out. A tooth grazed a leg and sliced it open.

Simon emerged from the tubing, his hind leg dragging. Pebhlo was behind and getting ready to pounce. Simon rolled to throw him off but he rolled too and managed to keep up. Again his fangs flashed and missed him by a hair — Simon heard them clatter together. There was an intake of air as Pebhlo lunged and …

A railroad tie came crashing down. It weighed fifty kilos at least but Gilles had thrown it effortlessly. Pebhlo's rat was in the way. It squeaked miserably and that was all.

With his vadh killed, Pebhlo was out of commission. But Serdho kept after Simon, twisting and turning in a way that wasn't human. His movements reminded Simon that he could push his vadh further. Focusing hard, he tensed the rat's muscles and, releasing them at once, jumped ten metres. Serdho tried to keep up, but Simon jumped again and again, until he reached an overpass and climbed its girders expertly.

The overpass led to Terminal Avenue, which even at that hour was busy with traffic. Three enormous rigs roared by, one with a Lab sticking its head out a window. Even as Simon considered his options, something struck him hard from above. What the...?

It was a gull. Pebhlo must have squeezed inside it.

The rat fell twenty metres. As he spun in the air, Simon spied Gilles waiting below. He was grinning widely. Realizing the rat had served its purpose, Simon deserted it and took to the air.

Regaining Terminal Avenue, where he could see Pebhlo turning the gull in circles, Simon saw the rigs that had passed just seconds before and shot off in their wake. They were moving fast and he had to hurry. Because of his shock and exposure outside, his kaba was weakening with each passing second. He pushed himself impossibly hard, shaking like a building on the brink of collapse. Just when he was certain his kaba would pop, he managed to duck inside the Lab.

The dog barely noticed and kept hanging out the window. Its owner, a beefy guy who smelled of cigarettes and beer, was humming a country and western tune, "I Walk the Line," one of Mrs. Carpenter's favourites. Normally Simon would have cringed at this music, but he was so glad to have escaped that he actually grinned.

Terminal Avenue ended and the truck continued on Quebec Street. Creekside Park appeared on the left.

While it didn't have a lot of trees to boast of, the ones it had were swarming with starlings. On impulse, Simon abandoned the dog and settled in a nestling.

He was one bird in a million and safe for the moment.

Chapter Eight

The bell echoed across the schoolyard. It could be heard in the playing fields, the Japanese garden with its bamboo bridge, and the parking lot and picnic area where students smoked when the coast was clear. The clangour even travelled to the streets beyond, straight into the thick of the tree where Simon was hiding in the vadh of a gull and keeping an eye on the approach to the school.

His old plan was pointless. Since leaving Henry's body, he hadn't spotted any shatl that he could take over. He hadn't dared look, in fact, because such bodies were uncommon and might contain a foreign spirit. After his close call with Serdho, he wanted to stay away from bolkhs. But that meant he couldn't visit his family and tell them how Cletho had driven him out. After all, how could he speak to them in the guise of a bird? For want of any other ideas, he'd decided to follow Ian and Cletho about. That was why he was by the school — he was waiting for them to show so he could watch them from a distance.

So, where were they?

At the same time, Simon needed information. There was more to this tale than the loss of his shatl. According to the talk between Serdho and Pebhlo, there was a meeting scheduled for later that evening, an important one by the sound of it. By tagging along he might learn something more about these bolkhs: who they were, what they were planning, and how he was connected to them. It might be helpful, too, to catch a glimpse of their leader. What was his name? Carhlo? No. It began with *T*. Tarhlo. That was it.

But how was he to attend this meeting? Vancouver was an awfully big city. The meeting spot was at a place called Koblansky's, but the name didn't ring any bells. Obviously he had to look it up, on one of the school's computers perhaps. Although this would be far from easy: his vessel wasn't human and he had no hands to work with.

As if to prove this point, Simon shifted his wings. They felt as if they were a part of him now and as natural as his arms had been when he and his body had been joined together. He was making progress with this transmigration.

And why not? He'd been busy practising these last few hours. After hiding among the starlings awhile, to throw any lingering bolkhs off his scent, he'd decided to test his talents out. Cletho had said he couldn't ride a vadh that was smaller than a mouse's, but Simon wondered if this applied to him too. Having taken over a mouse already, he'd been curious to see if he could control something smaller. He'd combed Creekside Park until he'd found what he was looking for: a Chafer beetle.

His dad was always cursing these pests because of the holes they left in the lawn. Simon's had been the size of a dime. Getting into it was like a man squeezing into a lunch box. He'd circled the beetle over and over, lunged several times and — the feeling had been crazy — wrested control of a leg or antenna. Then the narrow space had conquered him and forced him to back off. After failing five times, he'd tried something different. He'd compacted himself, over and over. His kaba, he'd discovered, was like a sheet of paper that he could fold almost without limit. In this new, compressed form, he'd "attacked" the beetle again. This time he'd managed to roll inside, with some space left over.

He'd become more ambitious. From the beetle, he'd packed himself into a snail — it had been like steering a bowl of hardened jelly — then an ant, a tick, and, finally, an aphid. And he hadn't stuck to animals only. By flattening himself as thin as a hair (that was the only way to describe it) he'd been able to merge with a tree, a bush, and a dandelion. He'd even occupied a blade of grass and laughed as the wind had blown him about.

All the while he'd been wondering where these powers came from and why his parents didn't share in them. Who was Simon Carpenter exactly? What was his relation to Cletho? Why could he project and not the rest of his family?

He shook himself and drew up straight in the tree. There — Ian and Cletho were fast approaching. They were running together and sharing a laugh, not caring that classes had started already. Looking on, Simon felt jealous. It had been a while since he'd made Ian smile. He often disagreed with Ian and they could quarrel over tiny things. But Cletho was treating him like a long lost friend and causing him to collapse with laughter. Maybe Ian liked this version of "Simon" and didn't want the old one back.

But these thoughts were unproductive. There was stuff to do.

Simon quit the gull and drifted to the school. He didn't feel so panicked now when he roamed outside a vadh or shatl. The choking sensation didn't hit him as hard and he didn't think his kaba was thinning. He really *was* mastering this projection business.

He shot past Cletho and entered the school through a window. Once inside, he toured the hallways, on the lookout for Sherkhan — the janitor's cat. Because Sherkan roamed the school at will, and entered class-rooms whenever it pleased, it was the perfect vadh to stash himself in. He explored the gym, the library, the staff room until he finally stumbled on the puss.

Sherkhan wasn't expecting him. One moment it was stretching, the next Simon was inside it. In a blink he commanded the grace and strength of a cat. But again, his vision was quirky. Everything was blurry, the objects near and far away. And while he could see variations of blue (the colour in students' jeans for example) the reds amounted to different shades of grey.

He set out after Ian. His brother was leaving the principal's office, where he'd received a late slip before heading to class. Cletho was with the secretary. Judging by her expression he was giving her lip. As Simon tailed his brother to the juniors' wing, he was thinking he would have to apologize for Cletho, if he ever got his shatl back.

Ian entered a classroom and Simon trotted behind. The students chuckled when they saw him dogging Ian and laughed even harder when he stretched out on a sill. Ms. Morris, the instructor, was teaching the Pythagorean Theorem. Simon yawned and groomed his fur.

His plan had been to watch Ian briefly, then proceed to the library to look up Koblansky's. But as Ms. Morris talked about adjacent angles, he couldn't keep himself from dozing off. He was exhausted and slept for forty minutes or so, awaking only when the school bell rang. For a moment he couldn't remember where he was. His kaba was bobbing against a windowpane, like a fly or mosquito trying vainly to escape, while a line of kids was heading out the door, joking and talking, and knocking into each other.

It's recess, he thought dimly. He'd drifted off and lost his grip on Sherkhan. The cat's kaba had resumed control and steered the vadh somewhere else in the school. Where was it now? He had to find it before …

Wait! His kaba! It hadn't thinned while he'd been sleeping, never mind it had been floating around outside. More interesting was the fact that it had dozed to begin with. If he needed sleep, the bolkhs would as well. But the crucial point was that he'd broken loose of Sherkhan. That had to mean bolkhs wandered when they dozed. In which case, Simon thought with excitement, he could watch Cletho closely and when his bolkh nodded off, rush his shatl and take it over. Well, well.

But first things first. He had to look up Koblansky's. Drifting off in search of Sherkhan, he found the cat in a distant hallway. Simon nabbed it but flinched as an unfamiliar taste struck home. Cat food. Yuck. Salty it was, with something sour mixed in. Wagging his tongue to get rid of the taste, he wandered past a mob of students, one of whom gave him a sandwich in passing. He licked it tentatively. Peanut butter. That was better than cat chow.

He moved into a hallway, which was crowded now. Everyone seemed huge, even the junior students. Manoeuvring between them was like threading a forest, only one with trees that were able to walk. It was a strain, too, to be craning upward, although the artwork on the walls, when seen from below, was weird and psychedelic, beautiful even.

The noise was awful. Each sound was strangely magnified, from students' voices to the echo of them walking. And music was bleeding from a few sets of headphones. Even in this muted guise, the notes stirred his nausea and made him feel dizzy. He wondered what would happen if the music were to hit him directly.

"Hey Dog Bone!" a familiar voice called out.

"Dog Bone! Wait up!" a second voice echoed.

Simon jumped. Peter and Winston. They were addressing him, or Cletho really. The hemindh was emerging from the boys' washroom.

"How's it going, Dog Bone?" Peter cried, blocking Cletho's path. Winston was beside him and clutching a laptop. Simon paused and cleaned his paws.

"What do you two losers want?" Cletho snarled.

"That's not nice," Peter said, his smile fading slightly. "We only want to tell you how impressed we are."

"Yeah?"

"You sure dazzled Ms. Guzman in biology class. How do you know so much about cavemen? Are your parents cavemen? Did you grow up in a cave?"

"Yeah. Sure. Look, nothing personal, but I don't like your tone. The same way I don't like this Dog Bone crap. Why don't you guys move along before someone gets hurt?"

"You know what, Dog Bone?" Winston said, handing his laptop over to Peter. "I really can't stand it. I'm gonna kick your ass to Hong Kong."

His fists were curled and he was ready to strike. Simon almost grinned. How interesting. He was hoping both parties would come off badly, even if it meant his shatl might get bruised. What a pity that, before Winston could pounce, Jenny Frobisher stepped in. She pushed him hard and he backed off quickly.

"One day your angel won't show," Winston snarled, "and you'll have to face me all on your lonesome."

"Big deal," Cletho said. "Whether I'm alone or not, you'll still be just a punk."

As Winston moved off down the hall, Cletho glanced at Jenny. "What do you want?" he asked. "A medal or something?"

Her reaction was odd. She looked at Cletho and her face went pale. Without a word, she hurried off, like someone fleeing an accident scene. She was easily the toughest kid in school, yet something about Cletho scared her badly, as if … no, that couldn't be.

The bell rang. Recess was over. With a shake of his head, Simon stalked down the hallway. While he was curious to know what Jenny had seen, he had to get that address for Koblansky's. He would solve the mystery some other time. A minute later, he drew up to the library door and meowed until the librarian took notice. A lover of cats as well as books, Ms. Lambert smiled and let Simon in.

"I see you have some reading to do," she joked in passing.

Little did she know.

He passed a line of bookshelves until he reached three tables that were crowded with computers. Each was taken — a few students were on spare and checking their Facebook accounts. If Simon wanted to look up Koblansky's, experience told him he'd have to wait a long time.

Unless …

He headed over to the Current Events corner. This space was removed from the rest of the room and was where Ms. Lambert kept the periodicals. It was a comfortable spot, hidden from view, and the perfect place to play a game of online poker, which was why Peter and Winston often hung out there. And, sure enough, there they were, seated at a table with a laptop between them.

They were eyeing the screen, entirely absorbed. Winston was saying how their opponent was bluffing and they should call his bet and raise him twenty. Simon leapt onto the table and bore down on their laptop.

"What the hell?" Peter cried, as Simon sprawled beside the keyboard.

"Hey, cat! Go away!" Winston yelled.

Simon merely glanced at them and hissed. They retreated from the table, leery of his fangs. Simon placed his paw on the mouse and moved the cursor to the X in the corner. He depressed the pad and the window closed, cancelling their poker game.

"What is this?"

"Hey, cat! You tired of living?"

Again Simon hissed and motioned with his paw, causing them to keep their distance. Turning to the laptop, he placed the cursor on the Google icon and clicked it hard. The search engine opened and he laughed within. Now came the tricky part ...

"Holy crap!" Peter spoke. "It can use a computer!"

"It's luck," Winston answered. "Hey, cat! I guess you think you're Bill Gates or something? Well, smart or dumb, we're going to teach you a lesson. Grab him, man!"

"No way. I hate cats. They give me the creeps."

"Yeah, well, I'm not afraid." Winston rolled a magazine into a club. He turned to Simon, grinning cruelly.

"You want to mess, cat? Well, you chose the wrong victim."

There are advantages to being a cat. Your control is so precise, your muscles and balance are so finely tuned, that when you're faced with a human, even an athletic one like Winston, you realize just how awkward they are.

"You gonna leave? No? Then take that, you ugly creep!"

Winston swung his "club" at Simon. Evading it easily — it seemed to move in slow motion — Simon lashed out, unsheathing his claws. He caught Winston on his right wrist and felt the skin give way. Instantly four lines appeared, each spitting drops of red.

"You freak!" Winston screamed, glancing at his wounds then waving his club. "I'm gonna make you history, bro!"

"Maybe that's not a good idea," Peter warned.

It wasn't.

As Winston swung the club three times, Simon ducked and jumped onto a shelf. Certain that he'd chased him off, Winston was about to crow in triumph, but that's when Simon lunged at him. Covering six feet in a standing jump, he hit Winston's chest and dug his nails into his shirt — it was silk and must have cost a miniature fortune. By twisting his front paws, he clawed the silk open and left eight lines on Winston's skin. As Winston spun about in alarm, Simon retracted his claws, dropped to the ground, and quickly resumed his place on the table. He hissed and spat for further effect.

"Let's get outta here!" Peter cried.

"That lousy cat! My shirt cost two hundred bucks! I'm gonna fetch a broom and beat its brains out!"

"Just move it, bro! He'll attack if we don't!"

When the pair left the alcove, Simon returned to the laptop. This was the hardest part. Gingerly he placed his paw on the pad and started punching out the different letters. Typing 'Koblansky Vancouver' took awhile, because his paw kept hitting several keys at once. When the words were in the search box, he hit Enter.

Thirty-four results appeared. There was Bill Koblansky Business Solutions, Paul Koblansky Interior Design, Sharon Koblansky with children's aid, Mike Koblansky and his big brass band, Koblansky Printers, Koblansky Linens, Koblansky Meat Packing, juggler Stan Koblansky …

Wait. Koblansky Meat Packing. What had Pebhlo said last night? Something about Tarhlo and the smell of blood? Simon chose this entry.

"Koblansky Meat Packing. Feeding BC families for fifty years. Located in Surrey, on 66th Avenue." His instincts tingled. This had to be it.

There was shouting in the distance. Peter and Winston. They were coming back with Ms. Lambert in tow. He closed the window and was about to leave. Just as suddenly he turned to the laptop.

He opened up Word. Manoeuvring his paw he typed a sentence. It wasn't perfect but his meaning was clear. He left the table and approached a group of students who would keep Peter and Winston from striking back.

What would they think when they saw Simon's message? It read: "dogbon says 'tings arnt alwys wat they sem."

Chapter Nine

The sun was almost below the horizon. A breeze was blowing in from the west, interfering with Simon's progress. It pushed him too far left, then right, then way too high, then in a downward spiral. And a bird had its eye on him — he thought it was a bird. Bird or otherwise, it passed him by. Whew!

He was in a common house fly. If a meeting was taking place at Koblansky's, dozens of hemindhs would probably show, some of whom might be keeping a lookout. It went without saying that he couldn't be caught. To prevent this from happening Simon had to hide in something small. A fly fit the bill, even if it posed problems.

To start with, his vision was all off. He was seeing lots of objects at once, none of which was sharply in focus. He could absorb light easily, even as the sun was setting, but couldn't interpret what his fly eye was seeing. He was relying more on what his own senses told him, a good thing too as he'd have been lost otherwise.

At the same time he was used to piloting birds. When the wind had struck his sea gull's wings, he'd known how to twist them and to coast just so. The fly was much more difficult to steer. Its weight was tiny compared to the gull's, and its paper-like wings were miniscule too. The slightest breeze could knock it off course. But it *was* more manoeuvrable: it could turn on a dime and perform loop-the-loops.

The worst part was his vulnerability. After leaving school, Simon had transferred to a sparrow, spent time in a raccoon, then hopped on board a sparrow again until, at 66th and the Pacific Highway, he'd boarded a fly. He was barely in it when a passing bird had nabbed him.

Being eaten was … uncomfortable. It was like a fist pounding down on him and bursting his vessel apart. The fly's kaba had dissolved, emitting a high-pitched shriek, a horrible, blood-curdling sound. Simon had felt bad for the fly: while small, almost trivial, its life had value, surely. As the bird had swallowed the fly's vadh whole, which had twitched and shuddered in a last act of protest, Simon had transferred to a second fly — the one in which he was travelling now.

He was nearing his objective. Ahead of him was a low, squat building that was a hundred metres long and had aluminum siding. There were vents at even intervals and, over to the back, a series of docks with retractable doors. Above a glassed-in entrance was a sign: Koblansky's. There was also a gut-wrenching smell in the air, of blood and guts and life cut short.

The fly's kaba was twitching. It found this stench exciting.

Simon wondered if he'd got the right Koblansky's. There was a stillness hanging over the place, as if the building were tired from the day's business practice, receiving carcasses and trimming meat off the bones. Why was it so quiet and dimly lit if it was the meeting place? Still, having travelled all that way, he had to look it over.

He landed on an outer wall, just above the entrance. Wandering over the aluminum surface, he drew near the roof. At a point where the wall and an overhang met he stopped abruptly. Just in time: an inch away hung a spider's web, with a large, hulking mass at its centre. Simon could sense the spider holding its breath and waiting for the fly to graze its strands so that it could pounce and strike out with its fangs. With a shudder of revulsion, Simon avoided the trap.

There. A gap in the siding drew him over. Squeezing through, he reached the cinder blocks behind. Searching out these blocks, he discovered a pair with crumbled mortar that formed a crack just large enough to pass through. Beyond these blocks there was a length of drywall. Simon found another tiny gap immediately beside an electrical outlet. A moment later he was in the building.

He flew across an office space. There was a cup with some drops of coffee at its bottom and he drank from it to give his vadh strength — the sound of the fly sucking was faintly disgusting. At the back of this room was a metal door. It was open slightly and he drifted through, somewhat apprehensively. What was waiting further on?

The answer came quickly. He was in a warehouse space. Some overhead lamps were on but the lighting was eerie. Metal hooks hung from the ceiling. Attached to some were carcasses of beef, suspended by the hooves. The skin had been flayed and the blood drained off. The bodies had been split in two, the ribs were visible, and the flesh was vivid. There were lots of carcasses, all hanging inert, the muscles intact but stilled by Death's wand.

Simon was spooked. He was thinking of fleeing when he heard some voices up ahead. So this *was* the place and there *was* a meeting. He inched his way forward bit by bit, flying a few feet then pausing briefly. After what seemed like an eternity, he reached a second room.

There were more dangling hooks, but all of them were vacant. There were also eight enormous band saws — to cut the carcasses, Simon assumed — as well as long tables with built-in troughs. There were hoses coiled all over the place and heavy metal doors attached to industrial fridges. In front of these doors was an open space. Simon gasped. It was packed with … weirdos.

There were just a few animals, otherwise the bolkhs were riding in shatls. These human "shells" weren't exactly normal. Most were like Henry, homeless boozers. Then there were some older people whose dishevelled looks led Simon to suppose that they had Alzheimer's or something like it. With their worn out faculties they'd be easy to hijack. Some children were present, teens as well, and a dozen adults in their prime. Simon was wondering how the bolkhs had nabbed them, until he noticed that this crew was dressed in hospital gowns. They were patients suffering from a range of ailments, madness, concussions, accidents, diseases, violence, and the occasional coma. The fly's antennae shivered all over.

As creepy as this setting was, he'd be wise to stick around and listen. He alighted on a ceiling beam, giving him a view of the proceedings.

"So, where's Tarhlo?" a hemindh grumbled. He was riding the body of a ten-year-old girl who was dressed in a nightie that was filthy and torn, a shocking contrast with its teddy bear pattern. The girl's stare was vacant and gave Simon the creeps.

"The wind will bring him. Be patient, Dohl," a huge man in an overcoat rebuked the girl. This figure had a hatchet face and hands that were grimy and covered in sores.

"Why should I be patient, Rahl?" Dohl complained. "Once again Tarhlo is like a charging bull, all madness and no wisdom. So a strange bolkh has surfaced. What does this prove?"

"You should speak less recklessly," Rahl murmured in warning.

"Why? I am tired of Tarhlo's promises. Hope doesn't feed the belly like meat. And other bolkhs agree with me."

His statement caused the crowd to grumble. Some hemindhs murmured their assent, while others, like Rahl, urged less dangerous language.

"Where is Tarhlo?" Dohl yelled above the hubbub. "If matters are so pressing, why does he linger?"

"He is coming from Chicago and beyond," a lady spoke. She looked like a grandmother, only her hair was tangled and her neck was fitted with a brace.

"And he has others to advise," Rahl resumed. "You shouldn't distract him when he toils at the hunt."

"I like that!" Dohl yelled. "He has missed the target ten thousand winters, and you dare suggest that I'm distracting him! If he were here, I would question him."

"And what would you ask?" a voice broke in. From the centre of the crowd a figure strode forth, causing everyone to gasp and murmur.

Tarhlo. He was riding the shatl of a man in his twenties, a tall, strong-looking specimen. He was dressed in a pinstripe suit, the sort of clothes an executive might wear, only some of it was bloody and a leg was torn. And when Tarhlo showed his left side off, Simon saw his shatl's head was badly damaged.

"You are a welcome sight," Dohl spoke, his confidence leaving him like air from a balloon. "And I see you are riding an interesting shatl."

"I found him a short while ago. He was struck by a car and pronounced dead by a doctor. He didn't need his shatl so I helped myself."

"He's … you mean … you're riding a corpse?"

"Yes. It is a talent of mine. But the corpse cannot be more than two days old."

The crowd was silent. The bolkhs backing Dohl were uncertain now, while the ones supporting Tarhlo were clearly pleased to see their leader.

"But you have questions," Tarhlo continued, in a tone

Nicholas Maes

that was friendly and at the same time dangerous.

Dohl swallowed hard. Tarhlo's arrival had splashed water on his rage, and Tarhlo had an air that wasn't to be toyed with. But Dohl's resentment got the better of him and, after clearing his throat, he spoke his mind freely.

"It is said you have summoned us because a stranger has appeared. Is this true?"

"No," Tarhlo answered. Then, in case the figures in the back hadn't heard, he repeated in a thunderous voice, "It is not true that a stranger has appeared."

"But the rumour …"

"In actual fact," Tarhlo went on, holding up a hand to keep people from speaking, "TWO new bolkhs have come to light. And they are far from normal. They are the bolkhs we've been searching for these last sixteen winters. Have you forgotten your joy when these saviours appeared and your misery when they were taken away, stolen beneath our very noses? Even as we despaired, I assured you we would track them down and, sure enough, that day has come."

Tarhlo smiled. The effect was ghastly. Even when he smiled, a corpse was still a corpse.

"Think what this means," he urged them. "The male is a woplh, according to Cletho. And where there's a woplh, there must be a *hamax*. Think of it, a *hamax*! After waiting bitter winters past counting, we have at last the means of incarnation!"

He paused. He was overcome with such emotion that his shatl was weeping tears of blood. Droplet after droplet spilled from his ducts, leaving stains on his ashen cheeks. But these tears weren't enough of a release. He flew from the shatl and circled the room in spirit form. Although his kaba was invisible, its life force was so explosive, so much like a shock wave from a bomb, that Simon sensed the course of its trajectory. It wafted close to the beam he was on and practically sucked his vadh into its wake. As quickly as he'd left the corpse, Tarhlo stole back in and raised its limbs from the floor.

The crowd was mesmerized. No one spoke. Even those who'd been impatient with Tarhlo were standing at attention, rapt and full of awe.

No. One was unimpressed. Dohl had lost his fear of Tarhlo and was making his hostile feelings clear. He was crossing the little girl's arms in defiance and holding her head scornfully high. When he spoke his tone was sharp, insulting, even though his shatl's voice was thin and reedy.

"Do you expect to sow hope in us?" he asked. "For centuries you have promised our lot would improve. A hundred times I have heard you say, 'This time we will be restored! Now the age of incarnation is near!' But always, without fail, we have suffered disappointment."

Dohl paused, as if daring the crowd to contradict him. When no one spoke, or moved a muscle, he nodded to himself and continued speaking. "It has been countless winters since the time of our expulsion. Untallied winters of waiting and false hopes. Whenever luras went to war, what did you say? 'This time they will destroy each other and we will feed upon their weakness!' When luras of the desert warred, of the rivers warred, of the wooden horse warred, of the great marble city warred, of the forests warred, of the castles warred, of the machines warred, of the hand-made fires and hurricanes warred, then, then, you promised always, we would rise, we would live, we would catch the summer breeze and have our retribution! 'Now it happens!' you promised. 'Now we will prevail!' But you were wrong. Always, you were wrong."

"Have you spoken all your words?" Tarhlo asked. His tone was deathly calm.

"No, I have not," Dohl answered. "When I decided to take matters in hand, and used shatls to crash the luras' machines, to jump from buildings and to take lura lives, you condemned my efforts, though they have proved successful."

"Your tactics were indiscriminate," Tarhlo observed, "and have not brought us closer to our goal."

"They were better than waiting!" Dohl exclaimed. Containing himself, he continued more calmly, "You would have my trust if your thoughts were true. You have spoken of a woplh and hamax. You say they appeared sixteen winters ago but vanished the very day they emerged. How many bolkhs can confirm your claim? How many saw this pair for themselves? And now you say Cletho has found them? Today marks the onset of our rebirth and we can achieve this by trusting in you? I say no! I say your reign has failed! I say the bolkhs should adopt my plan and we should use these shatls to destroy the luras! Crash their machines! Wreak death on their cities! Never mind the dream of incarnation! Let us forsake this fantasy once and for all! Let us soak our spears with lura blood and avenge our losses!"

"Now have you finished?" Tarhlo asked quietly.

"I have finished," Dohl answered, folding the girl's arms and staring at Tarhlo.

"Then I have two lessons for you, Dohl," Tarhlo announced in a mild tone. "First, I have never deceived the tribes. I have never spoken falsely. I have done what any leader must do when he rules a broken people. I have been what you are too small to be. I have always been hopeful."

"That's one lesson," Dohl sneered. "What is the second?"

"Bolkhs are not luras. We do not believe that we are equal. I am a Khalkon. You are a Threedh. Threedhs must yield to Khalkons, as nature has ordained. But you don't yield. And so a lesson must follow."

Tarhlo was so fast that Simon almost missed him. He grabbed the girl's neck and started to squeeze. Dohl struggled hard to escape but the odds were against him. His shatl was weaker than Tarhlo's corpse and he was no match at all for the Khalkon. The girl was gurgling and her face was blue. Her limbs were shaking and her eyes were popping. Not that Tarhlo intended her harm. It was Dohl and Dohl alone he was after. By stopping up the air supply, Tarhlo was rendering the shatl unfit for habitation. Sure enough, when the girl was near dying, Dohl jumped ship. Simon didn't see him leave, but somehow Tarhlo sensed the difference.

He released the girl. Free of any bolkh, she was preparing to scream. Before she could, Tarhlo left his shatl — the young man's body collapsed to the floor — and his kaba took possession of the girl.

"That's better," Tarhlo observed in her reedy voice, "A live shatl is more welcoming than one that's dead."

The girl shrugged her shoulders as Tarhlo made himself at home. She also lifted the corpse at her feet and threw it effortlessly across the room. It landed with a clatter against a distant band saw.

"Dohl!" Tarhlo cried, looking up at the ceiling. "You have no further role in our meetings. I hereby expel you from the tribe that raised you and refuse you entry to any of our councils. If any bolkh dares shelters you, converses with you, or aids your projects, he shall suffer expulsion as well. In the eyes of our people, you are dust, nothing more."

That said, Tarhlo looked away from the ceiling and stared at the shatls gathered about. Without a word, he studied each face, refusing to avert his gaze until each bolkh had signalled his submission. When all had offered their allegiance in this fashion, he finally spoke.

"Mourn not Dohl and his show of temper," he announced, his tone mild and controlled again. "A bolkh who doubts his leader is unworthy of his tribesmen, especially when a joyful day advances. Remember that a woplh signals an early spring, but a hamax marks a thousand years of summer. A new sun rises and incarnation is near!"

"Your words are comforting," Rahl replied, once the shouts of approval had died. "And Dohl was served justice when he rejected your wisdom. But can you tell us more about the woplh and hamax? Who are they and where can we find them?"

"Loyal Rahl!" Tarhlo laughed. "As always your questions lead us back to the trail. The woplh is at large and schemes for incarnation. His days are heavy with loneliness, I trust."

"And the other?" Rahl asked, with ill-concealed excitement.

"The hamax sits in a building by the sea. Her companions are luras who are weak with illness, while she glows with strength and health within. A true hamax, she will be the seed of our delivery. Think of it. Incarnation! Soon we will know true incarnation."

"Incarnation!" Rahl repeated.

"Incarnation!" the old lady spoke.

"Incarnation!" the others chanted, with incalculable yearning. "Incarnation!" they cried over and over.

Not that Simon stayed to listen. Already he had left the beam, was flying past the dangling meat and fleeing through the office space, past the drywall, past the blocks, past the siding to the night beyond.

The hamax that these freaks were after?

The target was Clara.

Chapter Ten

There was no one stirring. The streets were empty, the houses were dark, and, apart from the odd cricket chirping, the region was quiet. As quiet as a tomb. Simon wasn't surprised. It was 3:00 a.m. and the world was sleeping.

He was standing on the Carpenters' porch. After escaping from Koblansky's, he'd grabbed a pigeon and flown home. Just outside their house his luck had been amazing. He'd spied Henry in his shelter, sleeping off another binge. Simon had feared a bolkh had moved in, but on drawing close to the bum had found his "hollows" vacant. With a laugh Simon hijacked him, as easily as he might have tied his shoes.

Simon's mind was filled with questions. Who were Tarhlo and the bolkhs? What did hamax mean and woplh and incarnation? And, again, how was he linked to these freaks? The fastest way to solve this puzzle was to neutralize Cletho, regain his body, and prevent Clara from being snatched. That was why he was back at the house.

Three earthenware pots stood next to the door. He lifted the middle one and smiled in satisfaction: beneath it was a key to the door. Months earlier (it seemed more like years) he'd told his mom this hiding spot was obvious, the first place burglars would look for a key. He'd urged her not to place it there, saying he'd wait on the porch if he were ever locked out. It was lucky she'd ignored his advice.

He inserted the key and turned it slowly. A chuckle escaped him. He was part of the family and entitled to enter, but here he was, acting the thief. Still. All of this would change once he'd dealt with Cletho.

With the lock taken care of, Simon eased the door open and crept inside, being careful to avoid the third board to the right: it creaked when the slightest force was applied. Simon stood in the hallway and breathed the house in. Yes. He could smell his dad's aftershave, his mother's shampoo, the leftover tang of garlic from supper — Emma loved to cook with garlic — and the stench of hamster, from Magnus no doubt. An old-fashioned clock was keeping time in the background and the fridge was humming. He smiled appreciatively. He was home.

But he had a score to settle. Removing Henry's shoes, he shuffled forward in his stocking feet. His socks were full of holes and didn't smell so terrific.

He reached the stairs. By keeping to the sides and avoiding certain steps, he reached the second floor with barely a sound. At one point his foot struck a plastic sphere — it was an exercise ball belonging to Magnus — but he grabbed it quickly and stopped it from rolling all over.

Pausing on the second floor, he counted to fifty, in case someone was listening closely. Not someone — Cletho. For his plan to work, Simon had to catch Cletho sleeping, on the assumption his kaba would have drifted from his shatl. If so, Simon could win his body back, although he would have to be much faster than Cletho. If he were off by a fraction, his plan would fail.

He could hear someone snoring. The noise was coming from his parents' room, to his right, past the second-storey washroom. Ian's room was just to the left and, down a narrow alcove, was where he had slept. A night light cast an eerie light in the alcove. The door to his room was closed but that came as no surprise to Simon. If Cletho had, in fact, drifted free of his shatl, he couldn't afford to keep the door open.

"Let's do it," he told himself.

"*I've always liked pancakes*," Henry whispered from within. His alcoholic haze was wearing off.

Smiling at the drunk's remarks, Simon tiptoed to the door. He didn't have to worry about the floor making noises because it was covered in a length of thick green broadloom. He did almost knock into a ceiling fixture: Henry was tall and the alcove was low. He just managed to duck in time, and three seconds later his hand closed upon the doorknob.

The door was locked.

Simon had been expecting this. Inhaling deeply, he opted for Plan B. The door was fitted with an old-fashioned lock, with a keyhole that would admit a fly-sized object. By compressing his kaba, Simon could squeeze through easily. Leaving Henry's shatl behind, he floated to the keyhole and folded his kaba three times over.

Darn, darn, darn.

The hole was stuffed with wax. Cletho wasn't leaving things to chance.

Simon regained Henry before the drunk hit the floor. He stared long and hard at the lock. What was he supposed to do now?

"What's going on?" a familiar voice spoke.

Simon reacted with blinding speed. Spinning around, he lifted Ian and covered his mouth. Always feisty, Ian put up a struggle. He kicked and strained and tried to scream — to no avail. Desperate to keep Cletho from waking, Simon backed off from the door, retreated down the landing, and entered Ian's room. His brother was still twisting about.

"Ian," he whispered, pressing his lips to his ear, "I know this sounds crazy but it's me, Simon. My soul or spirit is stuck in Henry, while a stranger's soul has hijacked my body. Are you listening?"

Ian had stopped twisting and was lying limp in Henry's arms. He nodded to show he was paying attention.

"What's all that ruckus?" Henry spoke from within. He was two-thirds back to normal.

"Okay, good," Simon went on, ignoring Henry. "I can prove what I'm saying but I need your help. The stranger has blocked my keyhole with wax. Can you get me something sharp and thin, a penknife or a pencil maybe?"

"Is it day already?" Henry asked. *"Is the liquor store open?"*

"*Quiet!*" Simon shouted, then added to Ian, "I'm going to take my hand away but you can't make a sound because you'll awaken the stranger. If he's awake, I can't kick him out. Okay?"

Again Ian nodded.

Slowly Simon slackened his hold. He took his hand from Ian's mouth and set him on the floor. He patted his shoulder, to show he meant no harm.

Ian turned and looked at him. There was barely any light in the room and Simon couldn't read his expression. Maybe he believed him, maybe he didn't. Simon was ready to pounce if he screamed. But no. Ian went to his desk, rummaged in a drawer, and returned with a pen that he'd received on his birthday. It was an expensive model, made of sixteen-carat gold. Unscrewing it, he removed the refill inside and pressed it into Simon's hand. It was exactly what he needed to clear out the wax.

"*It must be mornin'. I'm feelin' peckish,*" Henry spoke. "*Besides a swallow of Jack, I could do with some pancakes.*"

"*Give me three more minutes, Henry, and I'll be gone,*" Simon said.

"*I ain't givin' you nothin'!*" Henry suddenly raged. "*You ain't got the right to be inside of me. Unless you got a bottle of Jack that is …*"

Ignoring Henry, Simon put his hand on Ian and escorted him out onto the landing. The pair approached his room with caution and, outside the door, he dropped to his knees. With Ian practically breathing in his ear, he fitted the refill into the keyhole and, as quietly as possible, started digging away. The wax-like substance broke apart in clumps. He removed three pieces and showed them to Ian.

But Ian wasn't there.

With a feeling of dread, Simon glanced around. At the far end of the landing, his parents' door stood open. Clearly Ian was cluing them in. In a minute all hell was going to break loose and Cletho would be wakened and take charge of his shatl. He had to get this hole unstuck!

"You hear me ghost?" Henry was yelling. *"You either give me Jack or get the hell out!"* The bum's kaba reared itself and gave Simon's a blow.

He dug at the wax. Another piece broke loose, and another, and another. Was the passage clear? No. He couldn't poke the pen through. From behind he heard his parents' bed creaking and ... someone was coming.

"I'm tired of being pushed around!" Henry screamed. *"Just 'cause I like to drink now and then don't give you the right to take my insides over! I order you to leave! You hear! You bring me Jack or ..."* He hit Simon's kaba again, causing him to slip half outside Henry's body — he felt as if he were hanging from a plane in mid-air. From far away, he felt the refill slip from Henry's fingers.

Footsteps were approaching, and he could hear people whispering.

Only with a burst of force was Simon able to return to Henry. He groped for the refill, as he addressed the bum, *"Why do you think I'm trying to open this door? There's Jack on the other side, not to mention John. Give me a minute and I'll fetch you both."*

"Why didn't you say so?" Henry grumbled. *"You have two minutes. And then you're out!"*

As he heard someone move in from behind, Simon picked the refill up. He shoved it in the keyhole as hard as he could. An instant later, he felt it give way. At the same time a hand descended on his shoulder.

"What's going on...?" his dad started to say, even as Simon abandoned Henry. No sooner was his kaba free than he folded it over several times, until it was small enough to navigate the keyhole. Manoeuvring past the remnants of wax, he emerged in a space that was achingly familiar. His desk, bed, and shelves were just as he'd left them, as were the posters hanging on the walls and the airplane models suspended from the ceiling. Over in one corner lay the cage from the pet shop.

On his bed was something even more familiar. His shatl. It was lying on its side, one arm trailing to the floor. It didn't seem to be moving at all, as if trapped in something even deeper than sleep. Was Cletho stowed inside it or not?

A knock rang out.

"Simon?" his dad called, "Is everything okay?"

Simon shot toward his shatl. If Cletho was inside already, Simon's kaba would bounce off; if he wasn't, there was a chance.

The next few seconds were very peculiar. His shatl did absorb him part way, a sign that Cletho had, in fact, drifted loose. But even as half his kaba slid in, an electrical bolt sliced right through him, as if he'd crammed his fingers in a socket. His entire kaba started to shimmer and he felt his essence grow thinner and thinner. And a force was dragging at him, like a magnet or …

Cletho. His kaba was fighting to win back the shatl. A second bolt ran through Simon, then a third, a fourth. His hold on his shatl was growing weaker.

"Simon?" he heard his father call, "Are you okay? Would you answer, please?" The doorknob rattled violently.

His dad's voice brought a realization home. This was his shatl. His. No one had the right to take it away. How dare Cletho run at him like this! A rage suddenly filled him and, on instinct, he folded his kaba over again. He felt Cletho pulsing nearby, his hold on the shatl just as loose as Simon's. He leapt at him in his compact state and delivered an electrical blow of his own, one much stronger than any he'd been given.

Cletho's grip slackened. He was one-tenth in and nine-tenths out. Simon hit him again. The bolkh lost his hold and flew across the room. With a pulse of triumph, Simon took his place of old — it was like slipping on a pair of old sneakers after walking miles in a pair of tight shoes.

"If you don't open this door, I'm breaking it down!" his father yelled.

His shatl enfolded him and he could move his limbs, as if he'd been connected to this space all along.

There was a thud and the door shuddered in its frame. His father was intent on forcing it open.

"Hang on a sec!" Simon yelled. "I'm putting on some clothes."

He glanced around the room. Cletho was still present. There was no way he could leave that space because the window was closed and the keyhole was tiny — too small for the likes of Cletho to use. With no spare vadh about, he would wither in minutes.

"Simon! Open up already!"

"Sorry! I'm almost there!"

There was a shuffling in the corner, from the pet shop's cage. Surprised, Simon looked it over. Oh. He should have known. Ian's hamster was resting inside, only its kaba had lost the use of its vadh: desperate to survive, Cletho had taken it over.

"Simon! We're worried! Open up this instant!"

"Not bad for a novice," a voice broke in. *"You've learned some tricks since I've seen you last. 'N you sure pack a wallop. It's lucky I kept dis hamster in de room, just in case I needed a vadh real quick."*

"You've been in touch with Tarhlo?" Simon asked, fitting the cage's lid in place.

"How didja know? Dat ain't none of your business!"

"I attended the meeting at Koblansky's this evening. Why have you sent them looking for Clara? What's a hamax? A woplh? And what does incarnation mean?"

"Look, bud. Ask no questions 'n I'll tell no lies."

"Listen…!"

"Simon! That's it! I'm calling the police!" his father yelled.

"You'd be wise to open. Dose luras mean business when dey get steamed up."

"Those luras are my family," Simon said.

"Whatever you say," Cletho smirked.

While he was dying to question Cletho further, Simon realized he couldn't keep his family waiting. Spying the key to the door on his dresser, he turned it in the lock. Instantly the door flew open. His father was standing directly outside in a ragged T-shirt and jockey shorts. His hair was dishevelled and he wasn't wearing his glasses — his puffy eyes made him look a bit like Magnus. Simon's mom was standing beside him, in a nightie that he'd given her on Mother's Day. Her cheeks were covered in facial cream. Ian was present and, at his feet, Henry — the bum was muttering how he was owed some Jack. Behind them stood Emma, her fists were bunched and she was ready for trouble.

"What's going on?" his father raged. "Ian said that Henry said you were inside him, while someone else was living in you …"

"First, tell me this: are you okay?" his mom demanded.

"And are you Simon?" Ian asked. "I mean, Henry sounded real convincing."

"Of course he's Simon," his mother said. "Who else would he be?"

"This calls for a drink!" Henry cried, propping himself into a sitting position.

"Quiet!" Mr. Carpenter fumed. "I told you not to bother us or I'd call the police!"

"Don't go thinkin' that you've won," Cletho jeered. *"We've got bolkhs who'll be watchin' your every move."*

Simon sighed. Where should he begin? How would he get his family to believe him? His father was an engineer, his mother a doctor: both believed in the majesty of science, not in tales about transmigration.

And then it struck him. His body collapsed to the floor.

"Oh my God! Simon!" his mother screamed.

"Son! What's wrong?" his father yelled.

"I'll call 911!" Emma was saying.

"Mom! Dad!" Simon called from behind, barely managing to occupy Henry, "Over here. Don't worry. I'll tell you everything."

Chapter Eleven

" . . . If we apply the idea of natural selection to our forebears, we see that humans are hardly special. Through the give and take of natural selection, the earliest mammals gave rise to the apes. The apes kept developing, or were naturally selected, and eventually an offshoot with special properties appeared. This in turn produced bipedal apes and, later on, the hominids …"

For the fifteenth time Simon glanced at a clock — it hung above a poster of Charles Darwin. He was sure the minute hand had frozen over, unless time itself had come to a stop. Maybe that was why the clock wasn't moving and Ms. Guzman was repeating the same information, how one group of cavemen had supplanted another. Here he was, on the edge of his seat, and his teacher was discussing irrelevant stuff.

It had taken time but he'd finally clued his family in, on Cletho, Tarhlo, the bolkhs, and his abilities. When his parents' doubts had come seeping back, he'd flown outside, found a raccoon, and proved to them that he was inside it. For her part, Emma had believed him straight off, as if she had already known how matters stood. She'd been terrified, too, when he'd mentioned Clara and how the bolkhs were interested in nabbing her. But again the news didn't shock her completely.

"… With the hominids, hunting came about and, with it, culture. This accelerated the effects of natural selection, and later hominids replaced the early ones: habilis, erectus, ergaster, Neanderthal, one arose from the other, through the forces of selection and hard competition …"

They were in mortal danger, Simon emphasized. Tarhlo was intent on snatching Clara and using her as a means of incarnation — whatever that meant. Simon was a target too. And to judge by his words and harsh treatment of Dohl, this Tarhlo was ruthless, lethal even. Because the police couldn't help them — how on earth could they protect them from spirits? — Simon's course was clear. He had to protect himself, as well as Clara and Emma. Simply put, they had to escape.

When he and his family had reached this conclusion, they'd discussed where Simon and the others should go. After they'd listed the possibilities — the countryside, the Maritimes, Atlanta, Georgia (where some relative lived) — Emma had disclosed the existence of a brother. For reasons she didn't want to explain, he'd been living in Europe for a very long time and been sending her letters all these years — he was the mysterious "boyfriend." She was close to him, in other words, and knew for a fact that he would help them out, once they managed to make their way over.

After another hour of heated discussion, Simon's dad had come up with a plan — trust an engineer to think things through. Emma would take Clara to join her brother in Europe. Simon would accompany them — he almost wailed when he made this announcement. The Carpenters would vanish until they were certain the others had left Canada; this would prevent Tarhlo from taking them hostage. And they'd have to act quickly, before the bolkhs swooped in.

There was a problem. As Cletho had warned, the bolkhs would be watching. For sure they were stationed nearby and would follow Emma when she stepped outside. If she weren't careful, she would lead them to Clara. And if Tarhlo learned they were aware of his plan, that his spy Cletho was imprisoned in a hamster, and that they were taking steps to safeguard Clara, he would storm the house with legions of hemindhs and stop them from fleeing. They would have to act as if nothing was wrong.

"… Do you see the pattern? Like time, natural selection never stops. It's always bringing traits to the fore and dropping others like a hot potato. It is the fundamental principle that drives evolution, and so long as there is life on earth, there will always be change. No species can remain forever on top …"

This was why Simon and Ian were at school, so the bolkhs wouldn't guess something was up. When the lunch bell rang, they'd leave the building with lots of students and avoid being detected if any bolkhs were watching. They would walk five blocks to a designated spot where their parents would be waiting in a borrowed car.

The older Carpenters had gone to work. In addition to packing their van with clothes, food, supplies, and camping equipment, they'd hidden Emma under a blanket to prevent the bolkhs from seeing her. Taking his usual route to work, Mr. Carpenter had dropped her off downtown. From there, Emma took the bus to East Vancouver, where she managed to get Clara released. From there, they took the SkyTrain to the airport and picked up tickets at the KLM counter, which she had purchased online the night before.

At work Simon's dad would switch cars with a colleague — he'd arranged this in advance — then travel to the hospital, where he'd meet Simon's mother. They would drive to a spot not too far from Simon's school, meet the kids when the lunch bell rang, and drop Simon off at a SkyTrain station. From there he would go to the airport and meet up with Emma. The Carpenters would journey to the Whistler region, where they would camp in the backwoods for a couple of days, allowing time for the others to join Emma's brother, whom she'd emailed the night before. It was an excellent plan except for one detail: Simon would be gone for an indefinite period.

What time was it? It was one minute closer to lunch, that's all. In some ways Simon wanted the clock to stay put. Once the lunch bell rang and they launched their plan, he wouldn't see his family for an awfully long time. In fact, he might never …

He had to pinch his leg to keep himself from crying.

—/—/—

Simon was roaming the school. Too antsy to wait for the bell to ring he'd raised his hand to visit the washroom, not because he needed to go but to stretch his legs and calm himself. He'd already walked the hallways twice and was rounding a corner outside the cafeteria. Someone was approaching from the other direction and he and Simon almost collided.

"Geez! Watch it!" Winston yelled. He was wearing a red shirt, a Yankees cap, and a pair of brown chinos.

"Sorry," Simon apologized. "I didn't see you."

"Dog Bone! You again?" While Winston practically growled at him, he was scared of Simon. That message from Sherkhan had him nervous still. His hands were shaking visibly, a sign he'd taken his Ritalin that morning. Simon couldn't help himself: he moved in and out of Winston at lightning speed.

"I have a favour to ask," Simon announced abruptly.

"A favour?" Winston laughed. "Why would I do you a favour? I hate your guts, in case you've forgotten."

"Because we have something in common, believe it or not."

"Yeah? Like what?"

"Your mother's sick. Her tests were positive. You're worried about her."

"Geez, you're a freak!" Winston yelled, shoving Simon in his fury. "And my mother's health is none of your business!"

"In my case," Simon went on, unfazed by Winston's show of violence, "I'm leaving on a long trip soon. I don't know when I'll see my mom again. It could be days, or months, or even forever."

Winston considered him. Across the hall was a concrete slab that the foyer's central pillar rested on. Moving
away from Simon, he sat on this block. After a second or
two, Simon joined him.

"It's the uncertainty that gets me," Winston said.

"Uncertainty's a killer," Simon agreed.

They sat in silence for a couple of minutes. Simon
was dreading the sound of the bell. When it rang, his old
life would wither away and something new would take
its place. All because he'd purchased a rabbit.

"So? Will you do me that favour?"

"Sure. What the hell."

"We'll be there shortly," Mr. Carpenter said. They were
driving south on the Oak Street Bridge, en route to
the Bridgeport Skytrain station. That's where Simon
would board a train that would take him all the way
to the airport.

"You look so different," his mother said, making
small talk to distract them from the scene ahead. "I
guess clothes really do make the man."

"It's true," Simon agreed. "I feel different in these
clothes."

He glanced at the red shirt and brown chinos he
was wearing. When he'd asked Winston to exchange
clothes with him, the guy had thought he was putting
him on. When Simon had just stared at him, Winston
had realized this was no joke and proceeded to the first

floor washroom. They'd entered two adjoining stalls and exchanged shirts and pants. Both had emerged from the stalls transformed.

Minutes later the lunch bell rang. As a horde of students had rushed the school's exits, Simon had tossed Winston a smile and joined their ranks. If some bolkh had been keeping watch, he would never have spied Simon in that heaving swarm. The same was true of Ian, who'd swapped his sweater for a hockey jacket. Ten minutes later they'd joined their parents in a large parking lot. His mother had looked silly in a wig, his dad preposterous in a weather-beaten Stetson. But there was no way they were being followed.

"We're halfway across the bridge," his father said. He'd been describing their progress in unnecessary detail, to dull the pain of parting.

"Have you got your passport?" his mom asked, not for the first time.

"It's in my knapsack."

"And money?"

"You bet."

"And you'll email us?"

"Of course."

"It's a good thing Emma has a brother abroad. I find it strange she never mentioned him, although it must have been to keep him safe. It's so crazy, all this stuff about bolkhs. If I hadn't seen your antics for myself, I would think you were insane."

"We're approaching Sea Island Way," his dad said in a mournful tone.

"When are we going to see you?" Ian asked. "How long will you be gone?"

It was the question no one had wanted to face. Two days before they'd been a normal family, "regular taxpayers" his dad had always joked, and now Simon was leaving without them, while they were hiding from a bunch of ghosts. They didn't want to believe this nonsense, but since Simon had addressed them from inside Henry, and assumed control of a raccoon, their hands had been forced.

"I don't know," Simon said, his voice cracking slightly. "It could be a while."

"How long?" Ian insisted, tears rolling down his cheek. "A week? A month? Not more than a year?"

"I don't know," Simon repeated. "A month, I hope."

"We're on the Great Canadian Way. The station's up ahead." His father had to focus hard to speak these words.

"When you do come back," his mother said, "you'll find everything in place, exactly as you left it. And we'll wait however long it takes. Just come back safe."

"Simon," Ian wailed, clasping his brother.

"We're here," his dad said, turning in his seat. "We should make this quick, in case those ghosts are watching. Son …" His voice failed and he was clasping Simon hard.

"Go," his mother said, her voice impossibly high. "Go and don't look back. Just remember that we'll be here always. Go. We love you dearly."

Simon left the car without a further word. Shouldering a bag that had been resting in his lap, he closed the door and started walking as his family pulled away from the curb. As his mom had advised, he didn't look back. He didn't wave and jump about and shout that he loved them more than he could say, that he was grateful for everything they'd given him, that he would miss them dreadfully, that he hated flying off on his own. They knew and he knew and ... that was that.

He climbed the station steps, taking two at a time.

The airport confounded him. The space was huge, ran on forever, and was flooded with soft, mid-afternoon light. It was built from sheets of glass and metal girders fused together in a complex array that reminded Simon of the Meccano he'd played with, once upon a time when life had been normal. There were works of Native art all over: he'd passed two totem poles, each six metres tall, and a large stone carving of people paddling a canoe. While these works were gorgeous, they made him feel empty. He was leaving everything behind, wasn't he? He might never see BC again, his family, the mountains, the beautiful sea.

Concentrate, he told himself. Lives were at stake and he couldn't go stupid. Focusing hard, he looked for Emma and Clara.

The place was hopping. The KLM counter was near the Air India one, as well as ones for Air France and El Al. There were hundreds of travellers milling about, and more were arriving with each passing minute. The air was alive with Hindi, Hebrew, French, Dutch, and English, and people were laughing and jabbering away or bawling their eyes out because a loved one was leaving. There was baggage everywhere and lots of kids. An airport guard kept telling them to take it easy.

Every few minutes a plane would take off with a roar.

Where the heck were they? It was 2:20 and their flight was scheduled for 3:15. They had fifty-five minutes to check their baggage, get a boarding card, and navigate security. To judge by the lineup, they'd be waiting a long time.

Something was wrong. Had Emma been followed, despite their many precautions? Maybe she'd been nabbed at the Dooley Center, by goons like the ones who'd gathered at Koblansky's, or by Tarhlo, who was desperate to get his hands on Clara. And if these ghosts had managed to capture Emma, maybe they'd nabbed the Carpenters too. Maybe Simon had no one left to rely on and …

He was sweating. It was odd that he could be in a crowd, yet feel like the very last soul in the world. He hated the thought of being alone. He could endure just about any hardship — hunger, cold, heat, and pain — so long as he knew that there were friends he could count on. Like that traveller on his right, an older man on crutches. He looked pale, weak, and on his last legs, but at least he had a wife and kids by his side.

Where were they? What was keeping them? In the distance he heard a plane taking off. It sounded like a dragon roasting its prey to cinders.

He was on the verge of panicking when the crowd split open and … there they were. Emma was holding Clara's hand … and accompanying them was Jenny

Frobisher! Spying him, Emma waved him forward. Normally expressionless, Clara smiled, and even Jenny looked more welcoming than usual.

Simon almost cried with relief that he hadn't been abandoned.

Chapter Twelve

Simon gazed outside and admired the view. They'd been flying for six hours and were cruising over Newfoundland. In their wake a tired sun was setting. The land below was steeped in shadow and the clouds around them were streaked with fire.

His mood was weird, partly because he'd been napping deeply and felt a little groggy still. He was sad, too, to be leaving Vancouver, his home, his family, his past … and why? To escape some crazy, half-baked bolkhs. But the main reason why he felt completely at odds was that he was trapped in Clara and seeing the world from deep inside her.

Before advancing to the airline counter, Emma had told him to abandon his shatl and hitch a ride with Clara. Simon had thought she was pulling his leg, but she'd quickly made it clear she wasn't. "It's all for the best," she said. "I'll explain why later." When he had proven stubborn, she'd shown him the tickets: there was one for Clara, one for Jenny, one for her, and that was it. If he didn't hitch with Clara, he wouldn't be flying. When Simon had protested he couldn't jump into Clara, not unless she was drunk or unconscious, Emma had advised him to give it a try. With a shrug, Simon had lunged at the girl, certain he would bounce right off, like a pebble hitting a concrete wall. He'd passed inside her easily, as if a door had opened.

And that wasn't all. Instead of landing in a narrow space and feeling claustrophobic, as had been the case when he'd hijacked Henry, he'd wound up in an area as large as a cathedral. On and on its hollows ran, seemingly forever. And while vast and empty and dimly lit, the space was pleasant and easy to move in, as fine a refuge as any to be found.

What did it mean?

And he hadn't been alone. He'd come across a kaba belonging to a human. It was timid and had drifted off when Simon had drawn near. In fact, it had abandoned Clara altogether soon after Simon was comfortably installed. Moments later he'd watched in horror as his body, seated only a metre away, had twitched and stretched and gradually stood, a sign the kaba had taken it over. He'd been furious. This kaba had no right to his shatl, never mind that he couldn't use it any longer. And Emma hadn't made things better when she'd placed a letter in the hemindh's hand and advised it to wait until the police showed up.

They'd passed through security and hurried to their gate, looking furtively around to ensure no bolkh was watching. It was only when the plane had left and Vancouver had faded to a speck in the distance that the group had finally settled back. To call less attention to the group, Jenny was at the rear of the craft, while Emma and Clara were seated up front.

Now that he had slept and they were crossing the Atlantic, Simon was waiting for Emma's explanation.

"*So ask her,*" a voice prompted him. This was Clara speaking. Simon was shocked. He'd never heard her talk before, not like this. She was a mute, as far as he knew, so how could she be speaking like a normal person?

"*You're right. I can't,*" she said, cluing in to his thoughts. "*Not if it means really speaking to people. But I can talk when you're inside me, or when I'm inside someone else.*"

"*I don't get it. What's going on?*"

"*Emma will explain. Ask her anything you want.*"

"*How?*"

"*She's been drinking,*" Clara said.

This told him everything. Emma was getting drunk so he could jump inside and converse with her internally. Wondering if the booze had loosened her enough, he vacated Clara and leapt at his nanny. Oof. It took him several tries and his hold was weak, but he did manage to break inside her.

"*Hello dear,*" she said. "*So here we are.*"

"*Yes.*"

"*Okay, so tell me what you want to know.*"

"*Everything,*" Simon gasped, struggling hard to stay in place. Still, the more she drank, the stronger his perch would become. "*Who is Tarhlo? What's he up to? Why's he anxious to kidnap Clara? Who are these ghosts? Why is Jenny here? And why couldn't I bring my body along? I'm leaving all my family behind. Why do I have to abandon it too?"*

"I'll explain what I can," Emma said gently, *"but there are many things I still don't know. And I'm afraid you're in for a bit of a shock."*

"I'm used to shocks," Simon replied. *"Look at everything that's happened."*

"Okay," Emma said, smiling brightly. *"let's start at the beginning. Eighteen years ago I was working in a Halifax store. One day a guy named Terry walked in. We got to talking and he asked me on a date. I was happy to say yes. He'd been everywhere and done everything, never mind he was barely twenty. We clicked and saw a lot of each other. In fact, a few months later he popped the question. Of course I accepted, fool that I was."*

She reached for her cup. Her hand was shaking and Simon held it steady, otherwise the Scotch would have spilled all over.

"Our life together was pleasant but strange. For one thing, Terry had peculiar friends: drunks, bums, and injured people. And birds, squirrels, cats, and mice were always lounging on our window ledge. Terry refused to shoo them away. But the oddest part was how he'd sometimes collapse. He'd lock our room and lie down for hours, his eyes wide open, his body stiff as a board. The first time this happened I was sure he was dead."

"Does this Terry go by the name of Tarhlo?"

"Yes."

"He's very tough."

"Yes. But he treated me well. Especially when he found out I was pregnant. He screamed for joy and danced all over and kept saying, almost drunkenly, that he'd been waiting forever for news like this. Our neighbours almost called the police."

The stewardess appeared with the drink cart again. Emma ordered a Coke for Clara and asked for another shot of whisky. The woman was startled — Emma didn't look like a drinker. Still, she poured the drink and handed it over. When Emma sipped it, Simon's perch grew firmer.

"Then the strangest thing happened eight months later," she said, grimacing at the taste of the Scotch. "I was huge by then, believe me. Terry served me lunch and I got all dopey. Thinking back, I'm sure he drugged my soup. I dozed off and … it's hard to describe, but I swear a ghost broke into my body. I even heard it speak from far away, 'You really do have twins,' it said. 'The girl must be a hamax.' When this spirit left, another came in, then a third, a fourth, and lots of others. It was like having a tour group stroll inside me. When I awoke I described this dream to Terry. 'That's the last time I serve you barley soup,' he joked."

"Where do I come in?" Simon asked. The tale was interesting but he was growing restless.

"I'm getting there," Emma said with a giggle. "I wound up giving birth at home. That was Terry's idea. He said he hated doctors and his friend would help. She was a half-dead hag with rotting teeth. She'd been tending me for six months and seemed competent enough. But I was expecting

*twins, on account of that dream. That's why I was saddened
when only a girl emerged. Although she was gorgeous, Clara
was, and alert and strong and very healthy."*

She sipped her drink. Simon couldn't see her face,
but he could feel tears were streaming down her cheeks.
He was worried she'd attract someone's notice.

*"I can't describe Terry's reaction. He couldn't sit still
and kept howling with joy, again and again, driving the
neighbours crazy. He even threw a party for his pals, the
drunks and kooks and homeless souls. Just think of it. I'd
given birth and his first thought was to whoop it up. He
even forced some booze on me, insisting it would lift my
spirits. It's lucky he did. Because of that drink I heard
Clara speak. Can you imagine? There I was, huddled in
a chair, when she addressed me in an adult's voice, except
that she was four hours old.* 'Mama,' she said, 'it's your
daughter speaking. Listen closely because this is crucial. I'm not your only child. You gave birth to a son.
He's floating inside me in spirit form. We must run
away. Terry is dangerous and planning to hurt lots of
people. Leave tonight and never come back.' *I thought
the booze was making me crazy, but she said it was pry-
ing me open, and that's why I could understand her.
Repeating her warning to run away, she persuaded me
to take her advice."*

Emma paused as some turbulence hit the plane. For
a moment it shook violently and a group of passengers
yelped in fear. Emma merely smiled and took her drink
in hand to ensure it didn't slip from the tray. When the
plane levelled out, she quickly continued.

"*I fled that very day, when Terry's back was turned. I phoned my brother Earl to explain everything. On Clara's advice I told him to leave. When Terry discovered that I'd run away he would threaten to hurt Earl unless I returned. I also told Earl I'd be in touch — through the* poste restante *in Montreal. And that was that. I slipped away. I flew to St. John's, Chicago, New York City, and crossed the continent in stages by bus, before eventually settling down in Vancouver.*"

"Tell me more about your brother. Did he have any kids?"

"*His daughter's with us,*" Emma thrust a thumb in Jenny's direction, "*but he'll tell his own story when we see him later. Let me finish up. You know the next part, how your mom and I met. She was driving late at night when she banged into a pole.*"

"You delivered me, sure."

"*Yes and no. I delivered the baby. As I held it, Clara spoke.*"

"How did you hear her?"

"I was drinking," she confessed. "*For the very same reason I'm drinking now. It was the only way I could talk to her. Anyway, she said we had to help her brother. If her dad tracked her down, he'd catch both twins at once. 'We have to save him,' she insisted.*

"*I asked her how and she told me to choke the baby — not too hard but hard enough. I told her I couldn't choke a baby, but she insisted. It was the only way for her brother to be safe. She said he'd take the baby over and no one would find him.*"

"Why would she say that? A kaba can't jump into a body that's full ..."

Simon hit upon the answer himself. Cletho had mentioned something about limnls, kabas who had taken over newborns. In the hour after birth, he'd said, a newborn is weak and easy to expel.

"Go on," he said. *"I understand."*

"I had no choice," Emma continued, swallowing hard. *"Clara was screaming at me to choke the baby before it got too strong. I told her I couldn't and she yelled at me to drink more whisky. I always carried a bottle then, so she and I could talk together. I took three swallows. The booze allowed her to control my hands and I watched in horror as they made for the newborn. I tried to stop them but they squeezed its throat. They squeezed and squeezed until the baby turned blue."*

"Is everything okay, ma'am?" A stewardess was carrying a bag for garbage. She looked concerned because Emma was crying.

"I'm fine," Simon heard her say, from a million miles off. "I'm just sad to be leaving the west coast behind."

"At least you have your daughter with you."

"Yes. I'm very lucky."

"And if you don't mind my saying, you've had enough to drink."

With a nod Emma lifted her cup and dropped it in the garbage. When the stewardess moved on she spoke again, *"I'll make this quick, before the Scotch wears thin. Clara was right, you know. The newborn was weakened and her twin slipped in."*

"What about him? The newborn, I mean."

"He was robbed. It wasn't nice but I had to put my son first."

"So his kaba melted? The newborn died?"

"No. Didn't you see him? When you entered Clara?"

Again the answer struck. The kaba inside Clara who'd avoided his approach? It belonged to the newborn. It had been lying in Clara all these years, since the night his mother had crashed her car. But if that was so …

It was as if someone had struck him with a brick.

"That means …" he whispered.

"I'm afraid so," she said. "You're not Simon Carpenter. You're Carl Kalkin. I'm your mother and Terry, or Tarhlo, is your father. That body in the airport? It was never yours to begin with. It was *his*, the real Simon, who, after years of waiting, got his property back."

Simon was reeling. He'd guessed that there were gaps in his past, but it was shocking to learn that the people who'd raised him, fed him, praised him, cherished him, loved him, these people weren't his blood relations. He shook his head. He wasn't Simon Carpenter. Everything he'd assumed about himself? It was false. All of it.

Emma was speaking in a rush, aware the booze was wearing off. She'd been hired by the Carpenters, who'd required a nanny and invited her in. Clara had lived with them the first three years. While Clara had many talents, she was far from normal. For one thing, she was mute. There was also a good chance that Tarhlo would find her and Emma if they were seen in public together. That was why she'd been sent to a home, on the grounds that she was severely autistic. This precaution allowed Emma to watch over Carl. The plan had worked for sixteen years, until Simon had brought that rabbit home.

"You have reason to be angry," she spoke from a distance as the booze dried up and Simon's perch started slipping, *"but my actions were designed to keep you safe. And even if Terry does catch us now, he can't rob me of the years we've spent together. In other words, I have no regrets ... no regrets ... do you hear?"*

Simon's grip was weakening. He still had lots of questions to ask — who was Terry, or Tarhlo, exactly? What sort of shatl had he approached Emma in? And how had a bolkh gotten a lura pregnant? But the booze had evaporated and she could hold him no longer. After circling the cabin a couple of times, he resumed his "seat" in Clara's depths and used her eyes to glance outside.

They were over the Atlantic and caught inside a cloudbank. It was difficult to catch their bearings, to tell up from down and north from south. The same was true of him, he figured. He had no idea what his next step was and no longer had anything like a home to return to. All his foundations had been upended. How would this end? What would he do?

"Don't worry," a voice comforted him. *"You're not on your own. Whatever happens, brother, I'll be there to share it with you."*

Clara. He nodded and felt a touch better. And before he could dwell on his worries again she started swaying back and forth, until the rhythm gradually soothed his nerves and bit by bit rocked him to sleep.

Chapter Thirteen

From inside Clara, Simon scanned the crowd. They were standing in the arrivals hall at Schiphol airport, after waiting an hour to clear Dutch customs. The guard had asked them the usual questions, the purpose of their trip, whom they were meeting, and where they were planning to stay in Holland. His tone was cold and officious until Jenny addressed him in fluent Dutch. Smiling in delight, he let them through. Simon was shocked. In all the years he'd seen her at school, he'd heard her speak a dozen words at most. Yet she spoke a foreign language. Go figure.

"So," Emma said, "where's my brother?"

Other travellers were being greeted by their loved ones. A dad dropped his bags to scoop up an infant. A small Chinese woman hugged a towheaded giant. Siblings embraced, friends embraced, spouses embraced, parents hugged children. A young guy, Simon's age, was greeted with squeals by his parents and siblings, as a dachshund danced excitedly around him. Inside Clara,

Simon flinched. He was thinking the Carpenters weren't tied to him now. That uncle who was supposed to be picking them up? Simon hadn't known that he existed until yesterday.

"I can't see him," Emma said.

"Me either," Jenny added.

"But I guess that's the point. He doesn't want to be seen. Unless ..."

She left this thought unspoken. Now that they had landed in Europe, their prospects seemed hopeless. They were far removed from everything familiar and had only four hundred Euros, which wouldn't take them far. Emma had a bank card and could withdraw cash from ATMs, but that would keep them going for a few weeks at best. The worst part was they were being pursued and would never know if some bolkh was watching. They were alone, vulnerable, in very great danger — and returning home was out of the question.

"Where is he?" Emma demanded with a hint of panic.

No sooner had she spoken than a figure emerged from the thick of the crowd. The man was common looking. He wasn't tall or short, fat or skinny, his face was bland, his bearing average. He was wearing a plain suit of clothes and toting a blue, beaten-up knapsack. Overall he was ... nondescript. If Simon hadn't been paying attention, he would have missed this gent completely.

"Is that him?" he spoke from inside Clara. *"Ask your mom."*

"She's your mom too," Clara replied. She squeezed Emma's hand and pointed out the stranger. Emma

almost screamed with joy. The man made eye contact, nodded curtly, then wheeled and walked off. The women quickly followed behind.

He led them along a polished hall, pausing at a flower stand so that they could keep up. He then passed outside and entered a walkway that, after a hundred metres, ended in a parking lot. He climbed a flight of concrete steps. When they joined him on the second floor he was seated in a Citroën, which was (if possible) as nondescript as he was. The group entered the car without saying a word.

"Welcome everyone," Earl finally spoke, manoeuvring his way toward the parking lot's exit. Now that Simon had a better view, he saw that Earl looked a lot like Emma. His hair was russet, his eyes a deep coral.

"It's great to see you," Emma said, her voice suddenly tearful. "I just wish the occasion were a happier one."

"We take what we get," her brother replied, handing money to a parking attendant. "But look at *you*."

He said this to Jenny who was seated beside him. Although Simon could only view her from the side — Clara was seated directly behind Earl — he could tell his cousin was beaming. He couldn't believe it. Jenny Frobisher was actually smiling! She was also squeezing her father's hand so hard that Simon could hear the bones crack. He was suddenly ashamed of his recent moping. This pair hadn't seen each other in over six years and had clearly had it much rougher than him.

"Clara, I can't believe how beautiful you look," Earl said, glancing into the rear-view mirror. "And it's nice

to meet you, Simon, assuming you can hear me, that is."
These greetings done, his expression hardened. "Okay.
We have a schedule to keep. I want to sleep near Paris
and the drive is long. I also have some errands to run."

"What's the hurry?" Emma asked. "No one's on our
tail."

"It's just a matter of hours," Earl replied, as he steered
them onto a smaller highway. "The bolkhs will have spotted Simon's shatl at the airport and guessed you boarded
a plane for Europe. Tarhlo knows I live over here and
will assume we're joining forces. I've studied the different
airline schedules: they tell me his agents will be landing
within hours, in London, Amsterdam, Frankfurt, and
Paris. Word will spread and things will get hairy."

"Hairy?"

"You'll see what I mean. Right now we have some
business to tend to."

He took his hand from Jenny's and focused on the
road. They had left the airport's precinct and were in the
country. The scenery was different and Simon looked at
it with interest. The land was flat (so unlike Vancouver)
and divided into tidy fields with lines of trees planted on
their edges, to act as windbreaks, Simon assumed. The
sun was out but there were clouds all over, big, white,
friendly ones. They crossed a canal — one of dozens.
The grass on its banks was lusciously green and home to
families of ducks and geese.

"Where're we going?" Emma asked.

"To Haarlem. It's close. After you phoned, I saw this
item in the paper."

"Oh? Saying what?"

Instead of answering, Earl motioned to some sheep on their left. They were fat, healthy, and contented looking. Emma nodded and said the scene was peaceful.

"That's the point," Earl explained. He wanted them to recall this sight so that they'd notice the change when things got hairy. "Our lives might depend on it," he added sternly.

"*I like him,*" Clara whispered to Simon.

"*I do too,*" he whispered back.

They left the fields. A park appeared, then a subdivision and a sign that they were fast approaching a town. Beyond the houses were four soccer fields where several games were taking place at once, with players tearing about in reds, blues, and yellows. They veered onto a boulevard, drove about a kilometre, then turned left again. They passed a sign that read Kennemer Gasthuis and navigated buildings belonging to a hospital. As Simon wondered what his uncle was up to, Earl pulled into a parking spot.

"Come on," he said, climbing out and motioning Clara to follow. He had his beaten-up knapsack in hand.

"Where're you going?" Emma asked. "Shouldn't I come?"

"Leave this part to Clara and me. Don't worry. This is necessary and we won't be long."

Earl took Clara's hand and strode away. He entered a building, consulted a map, and pointed out the section he wanted to visit — neurology. He walked to an elevator and pressed the up button. The doors opened and he stepped inside, being sure to draw Clara (and Simon) behind. The doors hissed closed.

"You're wondering why we're here," he said. "There was a story in the paper about a roofer named Crispijn. He fell from a building fifteen metres high. His body's sound but he's in a deep coma. So I was thinking ..."

The doors opened. Striding down a hallway, Earl came upon a nursing station. He smiled at the nurse on duty and inquired (in Dutch) where he could find Jan Crispijn. When asked if they were relatives, he answered yes. His bearing was confident, his manner engaging, so the nurse merely nodded and mentioned a room number. Moments later they were standing beside a horse of man.

"Go on," Earl said, disconnecting tubes and wires. "Exit Clara and take this man over. Although he's big for my tastes."

"Is this fair?" Simon asked, some seconds later. He'd stolen into the roofer's body and was speaking through his mouth. "His family will be upset when they see he's gone."

"We can't be squeamish. We're meeting someone in Paris tomorrow and you can't go in Clara's body. Crispijn will serve our purpose well, never mind his size."

"But to pull him away when he's sick like this?"

"Our need is greater than his," Earl answered, rummaging in a closet and pulling out some overalls. "On your feet and put these on."

Simon took command of Crispijn. Satisfied that the shatl was his to control, he rose from the bed and put his feet on the floor. It was like taking over a full-grown moose, he was so enormous. At the same time, deep within, he spied Crispijn's kaba spinning in circles. It was badly damaged, maybe hopelessly so.

He dressed in the overalls that Earl handed over. He also put a white coat on that Earl had "borrowed" from the nurses' station. It was a tight fit but would make him look like a doctor.

"It's the details that count," Earl said with a smile. "The nurses won't notice as you walk away."

Checking to see if the coast was clear, he pushed Simon forward, then followed with Clara. No one stopped them as they passed the nursing station, lumbered down the hallway, and rode to the ground floor. It was only near the emergency department that a problem arose.

A female paramedic placed a hand on Simon's shoulder. She pointed to a gurney on which a man lay gasping. She jabbered something that Simon couldn't catch.

"She says he can't breathe," Earl told him quickly, "and the other doctors' hands are full. This is bad. You have to act like a doctor until her back is turned."

"Hold me steady," Simon answered, as he fell to his knees. "Make sure Crispijn doesn't slip to the floor."

Simon left the roofer and jumped at the patient. The man was rattled but not unconscious, and Simon could only get a hold for an instant. This was time enough for the kaba to tell him, *"Bee sting. Allergic."*

"He's been stung by a bee," he said, returning to Crispijn. "He's suffering an allergic reaction."

"It's anaphylaxis," Earl informed the paramedic. "He needs an EpiPen straight away."

If the woman was surprised that Earl was speaking for the doctor, her expression didn't show it. Instead she rummaged in a box by her feet and removed a tube, which she hastily unscrewed. Simon didn't see her stick the man — by then he was exiting the building with Earl — but he did hear the guy ululate in pain.

"That took longer than expected," Earl said, as they advanced upon the Citroën, "But …"

"But?" Simon asked.

"Well done. Really. You saved that man's life."

They climbed into the car and travelled on. Emma was relieved to have them back and Jenny was giggling at Crispijn's size. She changed places with Simon so that he would have more room up front. The back was too small for a giant like him.

They headed south. With Crispijn's head wedged against the ceiling, Simon watched canals, fields, and villages pass, their every detail carefully arranged and not an inch of land being wasted. Earl knew the area well: without consulting a map, he zipped by lots of towns, Heemstede, Bennebroek, Voorhout, Waasenaar, the expression on his face anxious and alert, like someone who's keeping a lookout for something. Windmills came and went, the odd stone dike, and fields overflowing with the season's tulips, their colours like paint on an artist's palette.

"We're near the sea," Emma commented. "I can smell the salt air."

"We're heading to Scheveningen," Earl replied. "It's the seaside district next to The Hague."

"Why there?" Emma asked.

"Because I'm running short of funds."

The vegetation was changing: it was scruffier and less luxuriant. The soil was sandier and there were lots of sand dunes. They were passing yet more subdivisions, a sprawling golf course, another park, and a crowd of high-end houses. Even as he studied the road, Earl was keeping an eye on the sky, as if expecting it to open and something noxious to fall.

Scheveningen started. It wasn't large but was very congested. There were a lot of tiny red-brick houses as well as rows of apartment blocks. The residents were walking about in very large numbers. The schools must have finished for lunch, judging by the clusters of students outside. A girl caught Simon's eye. Because he was too large for the car, she laughed and pointed him out to her friends. He smiled and wished he were normal like them.

They turned onto a large street in the tourist part of town. The area was thick with hotels, restaurants, and souvenir shops. And then there was the sea. An exhilarating mix of green and grey, it was poised two hundred metres away, bathed in salmon-pink light. A few ships bobbed on it, freighters and liners. The beach was blinding white and beckoned to them playfully. But this wasn't the time for fun, Earl told them as he veered into a parking lot.

Before them stood a pavilion of glass, its front projecting forward in the image of an ocean liner. It had a row of doors and a neon sign that read Holland Casino.

"Why're we here?" Emma asked.

"I told you. I'm running low on funds. I'll take Simon with me. We should be gone forty minutes or so."

They left the car and walked into the building. Passing two security guards, Earl strolled across a tiled lobby and wandered past a double door. They entered a large room with a low panelled ceiling and row upon row of slot machines. The place was crowded for the early afternoon. A range of people were pressing buttons on the consoles and staring as the wheels inside spun at random. Occasionally someone would cry in triumph; more often the players would frown in anger, press a button again, and lose more of their savings. Simon noticed that no one was smiling. Even the winners looked apprehensive.

Ignoring the machines, Earl walked up to a wicket with thick metal bars. He placed a thousand Euros down and received a stack of green and yellow chips. Cradling them, he walked the length of the room until he reached the gaming tables at the back. There was roulette, blackjack, Punto banco, and poker. Depositing his chips on a poker table, he asked the croupier to deal him in.

There were five men playing. This was a high-stakes table and admitted bets of up to five hundred Euros. Earl anted up his fifty Euros, received his cards, and followed the action.

He lost two hands and folded on the third. The fourth hand cost him three hundred Euros — his two pairs lost to three of a kind. One white-haired player in a sailor's cap joked that he'd left Lady Luck behind in his car. The other guys laughed. The croupier kept dealing.

Earl won the next hand with a pair of aces. The next three hands were successful too: one pot contained over three thousand Euros and Earl bagged it with a full house (jacks and sevens). The next two hands Earl folded early, only to win three pots in quick succession. He checked his watch. It had been thirty minutes and he was getting antsy.

"Two more hands," he whispered to Simon.

The next pot was respectable and Earl won it with ease. The last was more challenging. All five were in and the betting was high. One guy staked five hundred Euros, only to be called and raised five hundred more. Three players folded, but not Earl. He bet five hundred and his bid was raised. Simon could hardly stand the tension. He fluttered off from Crispijn and studied the rivals' cards.

"He's bluffing," he whispered, returning to Crispijn.

"I know," Earl answered. "Luckily I'm not."

He stood two minutes later and gathered his chips. At the wicket he cashed them in for twenty thousand Euros.

"That should keep us going," he said, as they left the casino.

"I don't like gambling," Simon confessed.

"I wasn't gambling," Earl replied. "I'm a vrindh, remember? I can't leave my body like you, but I can read people's faces and know when they're bluffing. Keep this in mind."

"Why?"

"One day you'll be earning your money this way."

Simon was going to say something but his uncle told him to get in the car. Earl was running and fumbling for his keys. His expression was fearful.

"What's the matter?" Emma said, as soon as they were in. "Did you lose?"

"I never lose," Earl shouted, starting the engine. "It's them. It's started."

"What do you mean?"

"Tarhlo's agents have arrived. They've issued the alert."

Chapter Fourteen

"How much longer?"

"I'm fastening the bolts. Another two minutes. Can you last that long?"

"Yeah."

"I knew Crispijn's muscles would come in handy."

They'd been driving for two hours since leaving the casino, always heading southeast toward the Belgian border. They'd driven past The Hague without stopping, past Rotterdam and Dordrecht — its skyline hadn't changed in over three hundred years.

The charm of the scenery failed to impress. Everyone was nervous, including Earl. At the worst moment possible, they'd suffered a flat. To make matters worse, they had no jack on hand. Calm as always, Earl had asked Simon to lift the car. Once Emma and the others had climbed to the road, Simon (or rather Crispijn) had hoisted the rear off the ground. The problem was the group could be easily spotted.

"Are those cows still grazing?"

"Yes."

"They're not approaching?"

"No."

"Then they can't be hemindhs. Not yet at least."

"Maybe. Can you hurry, please?"

The alert was clearly on. Flocks of birds kept sweeping by at fifteen-minute intervals. Instead of flying high, they would swoop in low and cruise past houses, sidewalks, restaurants, stores, and cars, moving quickly but on the watch for something. When one of them stumbled on an object of interest, it would fly in circles and lead the other birds to inspect it closely.

Birds were just the start of it. Cats and dogs were on the alert: they were standing by the side of the road and eyeing the traffic, like cops on the lookout for potential speeders. In the countryside, livestock was gathering in the fields and peering into the passing cars — sheep, cows, goats, and oxen. It would have been funny had their purpose been different.

"I'll tighten the nuts and then we're done. How's your back holding up?"

"It's holding. Just hurry."

"And the cows?"

"They're still normal."

They had to keep moving, Earl insisted. A moving car was safer than a standing one. He'd been jumping between the highways and country lanes in an effort to avoid any major traffic snarls. If they got caught in traffic, they'd be spotted for sure. Simon had been useful. He would leave Crispijn's body for seconds at a time, launch his kaba into the sky, and scan ahead to get the lay of the land.

They'd stopped for gas. After filling up the tank, Earl had removed three bags from the trunk. Inside were changes of clothes and several wigs. He'd trimmed Jenny's hair and made her look like a boy, while Clara was given a mass of curls and an old print dress. Earl hid Emma beneath a woollen blanket, to make it seem there were only four of them driving. To disguise himself, Earl also put on a wig — the long blonde strands made him look like a rock star.

Their precautions had paid off. Despite their numbers and frantic efforts, the hemindhs had not been able to spot them. Two birds had shown a bit of interest. Earl had thrown the first one off when he'd swerved into a very long tunnel. The second had flown in front of the car. By picking up speed, Earl had crushed it flat.

"Okay. That's it," he said. "You can set the car down."

"Look out," Emma warned. "There's a cow closing in."

"Let's get inside," Earl cried. "But don't look as though you're rushing."

They climbed into the car and he started the engine. As they pulled into the road, a cow charged forward and raced beside them, craning its head to look inside. The car gained speed and left it behind. Emma was hiding, so it couldn't count their numbers.

"Did it spot us?" she asked, in a muffled tone.

"It's behaving normally now," Simon said. "It's standing still and … it's starting to graze."

"Thank goodness," she said. "It didn't catch on."

"Unless the bolkh left the cow so it can chase us in a bird or something," Earl warned. "Watch for any possible vadhs."

Simon kept his eyes on the sky. There was a hawk way above them but it was keeping its distance. He mentioned this to Earl, who glanced briefly upward, then shrugged and said the coast was clear. For now at least.

They kept driving. They were heading to the city of Breda, a short distance north of the Belgian border, but Earl was sticking to the country roads and what should have been a short drive took a bit longer. They passed a string of villages, Lage Zwaluwe, Hooge Zwaluwe, Wagenberg, Terheijden. The land was flat and given over to farming, which explained the stink of manure in the air.

"This is my fault," Emma groaned. "We should never have come and put you in danger."

"Nonsense," Earl answered. "If Tarhlo gets his hands on Clara, we're all in trouble. She stands a better chance of escaping if we work together. And you can take away that blanket now."

"And Simon knows the truth," she continued, ignoring Earl. "That the Carpenters aren't his real mom and dad. I'm sorry, Son. I didn't mean to trick you, any more than I wanted to stick your sister in that children's home. My hand was forced. I had to save you from Tarhlo."

While he was still reeling from the news that Emma was his mother, Simon didn't blame her. Her hand *had* been forced and she'd been acting in his interest. He was just about to say as much when, rounding a corner, Earl hit the brakes hard.

Dead ahead a truck was in the road. The delivery van was on its side, bleeding smoke from its hood and belly and blocking the path.

"What now?" Earl grumbled.

He cut the engine and left the car, again taking his knapsack with him, and removing his wig so he wouldn't look ridiculous. Simon was behind him, in case he needed help. The pair approached the driver of the van. The guy was standing by the front of the truck, rubbing his neck and staring down at a sow. It was pink, maybe six feet long, and weighed two hundred kilos at least. It was also dead and bleeding profusely.

"That pig crossed the ditch and ran into my truck," he said in Dutch, after reassuring Earl that he was okay. "I got the idea she was tired of living, poor thing."

Earl smiled and asked if he wanted a lift. The guy said no, he'd radioed in and help was on its way. But the tow truck wouldn't come for an hour and he didn't think their car could pass.

Earl asked if they could try shifting the van. The driver said it couldn't hurt, so the three of them stood by the front of the truck and pushed and heaved for all they were worth. Simon was standing next to the sow and spied its guts and eyes' blank stare. He felt bad that its life had been wrested away. He also felt a very vague itching, but before he could investigate, the truck budged slightly.

"Keep shoving!" Earl encouraged him. "We need three more inches."

Simon kept straining. He felt as if his sinew would burst, but after a couple more shoves they moved the truck further. And whatever that itching was, it had vanished somehow.

"That's it," Earl said. "There's enough room to pass."

Bidding the driver good luck, they returned to the car. Earl engaged the engine and manoeuvred their car around the truck. A minute later they were on their way, heading down the road at a healthy pace. No one said a word. They were thinking that this crash was planned, that the pig had deliberately struck the truck, and that they were now on Tarhlo's radar.

But there was nothing. The sky was clear and the livestock around them were only interested in grazing. When Emma asked if this stillness was a bad sign, Earl laughed and squeezed his sister's knee. "If it is," he said, "I hope we have more bad signs like it. That pig was no kamikaze pilot — he was just an animal whose luck had run out."

Fifteen minutes later they were on the outskirts of Breda, passing a row of residential buildings. They came upon an open square with a dozen tables and chairs around it, and a trailer to the side. It was a food stand offering a variety of snacks: croquettes, meatballs, French fries, and the like. On impulse, Earl pulled into a drive and suggested that they eat something. Because it was well past three and they hadn't eaten since breakfast, everyone thought it was a great idea. He parked the car and clambered out, being sure to bring his knapsack with him. There was music blaring from a pair of speakers. Simon experienced a wave of nausea. His uncle had a word with the owner and the guy agreed to turn the music off.

They were soon devouring plates of food. Simon was ploughing through six hefty meatballs and thinking he could eat another three servings. It came as no surprise that Crispijn's appetite was huge. At the same time he was staring at the buildings around them and trying to ignore a feeling of discomfort. That itching had started up again and had spread to his legs, lower back, and torso. Crispijn was allergic to the overalls most likely. As soon as he was able to, he'd change his clothes.

A scream erupted. The group dropped their forks in panic. Ten metres away stood a modest playground, with three swings, a teeter totter, and a spiral slide. Beside the slide a man was standing over a boy. He was shaking the kid's arm and yelling in anger. The boy was tearful and very scared. He was maybe six years old.

"What's going on?" Simon asked.

"Never mind," Earl answered. "It's none of our business."

The man hit the boy a couple of times. Slap! Slap! Slap! The boy was shrieking.

"Now it is," Simon growled, rising to his feet.

When the man saw him approach, he backed off quickly and said something in Dutch. Simon stood between him and the boy. He heard Emma call to him, "Is this a good idea?" As the man kept blathering, Simon turned to the boy and stroked his arm, to assure him he was there to help. That's when he noticed the boy's skull was scarred, his eyes were feverish, and his arms were scabby. What…? The kid had suddenly grabbed his wrist. He was insanely strong and started wrestling Simon.

"So it is you," the boy spoke with a cackle. His voice was high-pitched, but contained something else … a note of aggression. By then the man had joined in and knocked Simon to his knees. The boy jumped on Simon and was starting to choke him. For all Crispijn's strength, his vadh was growing weaker. Simon's sight was dimming and the background sounds were fading, the passing cars, Emma's screams, the boy's crazy giggles. In a panic, Simon realized Crispijn was fainting.

A *zssst* ripped the air — it sounded like a bee whizzing by. The boy's grip slackened. A second *zssst* sounded, as if the air was catching fire, and the man fell back a couple of metres. Shaking his head to clear his senses, Simon staggered to his feet. The boy lunged forward again but a third *zssst* stopped him.

"Let's go," Earl said, leading Simon away. He was holding a rod that was forked at its tip. Simon wanted to ask what it was, but Earl yanked him aside.

The boy was limping toward them again. *Zssst.* Earl zapped his ribs and knocked him clean off his feet. The kid hit the slide and didn't rise this time.

"One zap usually does it," he mused. "Especially on children."

"You didn't kill them?" Simon asked, as they were off and running.

"This is a cattle prod," Earl said. "They've been stunned, nothing more. But we have to get away from here and … you can drive, can't you?"

"I don't have a licence but yeah …"

"Climb into the driver's seat and let's get going!" He handed him the car keys.

The women were in the car already, white with tension. Simon jumped behind the wheel and thrust the key in the ignition. He started the engine and pulled into the lane. He was going to say he wasn't permitted to drive because his father thought he was too distracted, but he grasped that his lack of attention had been a heightened state of awareness all along. He could drive — masterfully at that. Veering onto the main road, he wondered why Earl had given him the wheel.

"I knew it!" Earl said, fumbling in his knapsack. A moment later he'd extracted a gun.

"Where did that come from?" Emma cried.

"Relax. It's just an air pistol. I keep it around for pest control. Although this won't be easy. Keep it steady if you can," he advised Simon.

Earl rolled his window down and leaned his head out. In the rear-view mirror, Simon spotted his target: two pigeons were flying directly behind them. The bolkhs had left the man and child and hijacked the pigeons to track their quarry. Within minutes the group would have a flock to deal with, then cats, dogs, and humans as well.

Simon heard a soft thud.

"That's one down," Earl murmured, with a note of triumph.

Simon saw a pigeon fall to the road. He heard a metallic clack as his uncle reloaded. He pictured the bird's kaba, the shock to its system, and its spasms as the pellet had ripped it apart. What a pity. What a brutal thing it was that one kaba's survival meant the death of another.

"Damn it!" Earl cursed, firing again but missing by a hair. There was another clack as he inserted a third pellet.

Simon glanced ahead. They were coming to a stadium where a crowd had gathered. If they spotted Earl's gun they might get the wrong impression — they might call the cops and that could prove disastrous. For his part, Earl was aware of the crowd but it didn't seem to faze him. Concentrating hard, he aimed the pistol.

"Got it!" he cried, with a note of triumph. "Pull into the stadium — there's an entrance coming up. There. Now go to the underground parking lot — do you see the sign? Good. Nice driving by the way."

A minute later they were parked in the garage. Earl ordered everyone out of the car. With his knapsack in hand, he ducked into the shadows. The others waited in silence. This underground lot had a menacing feel. The cars seemed to be looking them over, as if the bolkhs had taken control of them too. The darkness was like a cloud of poison gas. Simon wasn't the only one spooked. Jenny was biting her nails.

A horn sounded suddenly, causing them to jump. Rounding a corner, Earl stopped before them, at the wheel of a dark-green Fiat sedan. He signalled them to take a seat. As soon as they were in he was off and rolling.

They drove a distance without anyone speaking. Simon was wondering about the struggle they faced. Was it worth it? Really? Over the last eight hours they'd taken over a sick man, gambled at cards with an unfair advantage, zapped two people (one of them a child), shot two pigeons, and stolen a car. Were these actions truly justified? How far could they go to ensure their own safety?

Earl caught his eye. His glance said everything. They had nothing to be sorry for. If pushed, he was prepared to go a lot farther.

He drove aggressively. Leaving Holland behind, they crossed into Belgium and sped toward the Antwerp region. Earl used his skills again and swapped the Fiat for a blue Volkswagen. By then the sun was on the horizon and they were grateful for the deepening shadows. They would be much harder to track in the dark, especially if they stuck to the highway.

Earl pushed on into the heart of the night. He went by Antwerp, Brussels, Mons, and a huge tract of farmland. They crossed into France and passed a dozen towns where battles had been fought during the First World War, involving the deaths of thousands — millions. This landscape hardly cheered them up.

Just as exhaustion was creeping in they reached the outskirts of a place called Compiègne, where, after navigating a maze of roads, they pulled into a lane that led to a farmhouse. Earl had rented this place for a week and laid-in a generous store of supplies, food, blankets, tools, and the like.

"That's better," Emma sighed, collapsing on a mattress.

"Don't get too comfortable," her brother warned. "We should be ready to leave at a moment's notice."

"Why? How long do you think we're going to wander?"

"How long?" Earl laughed, with genuine amusement. "We'll be wandering like this for the rest of our lives!"

Chapter Fifteen

"It's amazing, isn't it? Now you know why it's called the City of Light."

"I never thought a city could be so grand."

"Look all you want. But keep an eye out for Michel. He said he'd be wearing a dark-blue blazer."

Simon and Earl were in the heart of Paris. They were seated on a stone bench in the Jardin des Plantes, not far from the Natural History Museum. In the distance they could hear the muted blast of horns as a stream of cars navigated the city's Left Bank. By looking north, above some trees, Simon could see the spire of Notre Dame Cathedral.

They'd risen before sunrise. After a hasty breakfast and a chat with the girls they'd climbed into the car. The plan was to drive to the city centre where they would meet a guy who could tell them what Tarhlo was up to. Earl hated leaving the girls behind, but he figured it was safer this way. Paris is full of drunks and addicts, any one of whom could be recruited by Tarhlo. If he and

Simon were trapped by these hemindhs, the girls would still be free of their clutches. They'd been told to call a cab and leave the farmhouse if the men weren't back by eight that evening.

Earl had also given Emma a cellphone. It was new and linked to the phone in his pocket. But she was to use it only in a moment of crisis. "A moment of crisis," he reminded her sternly.

Just before Simon had entered the car, Jenny had asked him to do something strange. "Jump inside me," she'd prompted him. "You'll bounce right off but I have my reasons." While her request was odd, Simon had complied and leapt at her a couple of times. On the third attempt he'd squeezed a good way in, to the point where he'd been able to glimpse her kaba, only to be ejected with near painful violence. Jenny had been satisfied. When pressed to explain she said, "You'll remember me if I leave any clues behind."

The drive to Paris had been uneventful. Simon had asked if they could buy him some clothes; his skin still itched and was driving him crazy. If he could swap his overalls for something else perhaps the itch would go away. Earl had promised to visit a store in the city.

"So where is he?" Earl fretted, even though it wasn't yet noon. While his uncle had great qualities, patience wasn't one of them.

"How did you meet this guy?" Simon asked, squirming on the park bench. The itch was super irritating.

"We met in Vienna. He seemed normal enough but I knew he was a vrindh. Not only that, it turned out he was married to my wife's first cousin. Like me, he was forced to leave everything behind. We exchanged cell numbers and have been in touch ever since. The last time we spoke was two weeks ago — he said he'd discovered something huge. That's why I think he can answer your questions."

"Haarlem, Paris, and now Vienna. Have you really travelled everywhere in Europe?"

"I've been moving about for seventeen years, to avoid being nabbed by Tarhlo and his goons. I've been all over."

"Why is Tarhlo interested in you?"

"You still don't know?"

Some bells started ringing, startling Earl. He jumped and assumed a combat position. Realizing they were sounding the noon hour, he smiled and relaxed. Simon listened closely. While he hated music, these chimes were almost charming and distracted him from his dreadful itching. They really had to stop off for a new set of clothes!

"It's because of me," Earl said, sitting when the bells had stopped, "that Terry Kalkin pursued my sister — Terry is Tarhlo, as you probably know. Years ago I met a woman named Dolly. We got married and had a child."

"Jenny."

"Yeah. Well, two years later Emma weds Terry and, shortly after, gets herself pregnant. So far, so good. Then she phones just after she's given birth and tells this cockamamie story, how her baby daughter spoke to her and was hiding her twin brother inside. She also said that Terry was out to hurt lots of people. So she's running off, she says, and will write from the road. 'You have to escape too,' she warns before hanging up."

"You didn't believe her."

"Are you kidding? I thought she was nuts! Until I told Dolly. When I explained the story, she burst into tears. That's when I discovered my wife wasn't human, but a freak of nature called a limnl."

"A bolkh who's hijacked a newborn. Like me."

"Like you, exactly. But it turned out I wasn't normal either. If I were we'd never have had Jenny together. I was a vrindh, she told me, an incarnated bolkh. Bolkhs and humans can never have children, not even if the bolkh appears in a body, but vrindhs and bolkhs, well, that's a different story. This is why Terry courted my sister. He and Dolly are distant cousins. When he'd found out Dolly had gotten pregnant by me, he figured there was a chance that my sister was a vrindh as well. So he borrowed a body and poured on the charm. And there was more: Dolly said that Terry hated humans — luras they call them. For centuries, millennia, he'd been plotting against them and now, at last, because of Emma's twins, his chance had come to do something terrible."

"How?"

"Dolly didn't know. But the threat was real, so we ran for our lives. When Terry found out Emma was gone he'd have taken us hostage to lure her back. He'd have tortured us too, if it served his purpose. Dolly was scared, and she didn't scare easy. So there you have it. In the space of maybe fifteen minutes I went from being a happy guy to someone who'd be running for the rest of his life."

He stood and some bills slipped out of his pocket — part of his winnings from the Holland Casino. He'd given Emma half, in case the girls had to manage on their own. Chuckling at his carelessness he tucked the cash into his knapsack.

"There's not a lot to add," he went on. "We wandered the continent for ten long years. Name a place in North America and chances are I've seen it. But eventually we got careless. Stupidly we bought Jenny a dog. A bolkh took it over and we failed to notice. He found out who we were and reported us to Tarhlo, who hadn't tracked down Emma yet. By then he'd tortured all of Dolly's clan, cousins, aunts, uncles — everyone."

"Is that why Michel left his old life behind?"

"Yes."

"So how did you escape?"

"It was Dolly's doing. She fought Tarhlo off while I rescued Jenny. He murdered her, you know. He killed her shatl in the back of a truck and wouldn't let her kaba go. She died within minutes."

For a moment, Earl's face dissolved. Just as quickly, he regained control and plunged on with his story. "After that, I split up with Jenny, only because she'd be safer that way. I rented her a place in Vancouver. That's why she attended your school. I came here — I've always loved Europe. Since then I've been hopping all over the place. It's tiring to be moving always, but I suppose it beats being murdered by Tarhlo."

The day was hot but Simon felt chilled. He didn't mind that Emma was his mom. She'd been there for him always and was kind and loving. But Tarhlo? What a brute. Why did that thug have to be his father?

"There's Michel," Earl said, breaking in on Simon's thoughts. "And he's brought his daughter with him." He nodded toward a man who was standing a short way off. Like Earl, he blended in: his suit was plain, his posture stooped, his features bowed and nondescript. The same was true of the girl beside him. She was dressed in jeans and a dark-brown sweater. Neither one approached or signalled that they'd seen them. Michel only glanced at his watch and walked off quickly, like a man in a hurry to return to the office.

Earl went after them, but made sure to keep his distance, and Simon followed suit. Navigating the path, they veered to their left and entered an open area that was filled with plants of every size and description. To their right was an old-fashioned greenhouse, crammed with trees from tropical climes. It was as if a jungle had taken root inside it. They turned right and approached a huge stone building with oblong windows, sculptures all over, and an ornate black roof. Like everything in Paris, it was oversized and centuries old.

Michel and his daughter climbed a wide flight of stairs and passed behind two wooden doors. A plaque revealed this building was the Great Gallery of Evolution. Earl and Simon swiftly followed.

A cavernous room received them. It was packed with animals (stuffed of course): giraffes, apes, zebras, elephants, the list rolled on and on. There were also cabinets on the side of the room, exhibits with bones of all shapes and sizes, and stairs that led to a second-storey catwalk. The space was stunning: it had a gleaming wooden floor and was drowning in sunlight. But was it Simon's imagination or were the animals watching? Never mind that they were too far gone for bolkhs to take them over. Michel must have felt the same because he climbed some stairs and hurried past a door, as if he were anxious to put the hall behind him. His daughter didn't stray from his side. Weaving their way past a knot of tourists, Earl and Simon followed close behind.

After drifting through a network of rooms, each with cabinets of beasts on display, Michel stopped in a chamber full of bones. Along one wall was a row of human skeletons, only their dimensions seemed a touch smaller than normal. The skulls weren't typically human either and the jaws were heavier, less elegant looking. A large case showed five skeletons in a ring, their arms upraised as if they were casting a spell.

Michel turned to face them. "The answers you've been looking for are here," he said, without bothering to introduce himself or the girl.

"Hello, Michel," Earl replied. "You always get to the point, don't you?"

"I don't get it," Simon said. "Why am I looking at a lot of old bones?"

"These bones," Michel said, tapping a case with a finger, "belong to a hominid called Neanderthal man. He was a master hunter and ruled all of Europe for a hundred thousand years. Unfortunately a competitor happened along, Cro-Magnon man, or Homo sapiens sapiens.

Because his body was a bit more advanced, or his mind was sharper, Cro-Magnon slowly ousted Neanderthal. He multiplied and gave rise to us, the people who would farm, give rise to cities, and, further down the road, produce planes and computers; but the Neanderthals didn't fare so well. As far as we can tell, they became extinct."

"We studied evolution in school," Simon said, "but I don't see how …"

"I was in Spain last month," Michel went on, "to visit several caves full of prehistoric paintings. While touring them, I discovered something. In a complex that belonged to Neanderthal man — where these same skeletons were found — I came across these pictures. Take a look."

He handed several photographs over. Earl and Simon peered at them. They were pictures of hunting scenes that had been masterfully drawn, showing elks and bears surrounded by spearmen. But there was something else. Three photos showed scenes of a hunter with a spectre floating out of his body. There were also drawings of elks, wolves, and bears with man-like shadows inside, like they'd been taken over. The message was clear.

"Incredible," Earl said, handing the photos to Michel.

"Wait a second," Simon said, "are you saying the Neanderthals mastered transmigration? And that the bolkhs date back to Neanderthal times?"

"That's exactly what I'm saying." Michel stared at the skulls before him. They seemed to be grinning, as if they were hiding some secret. "Cro-Magnon was more advanced than Neanderthal. He could out-think him, outfight him, and easily out-hunt him. Over time, the

Neanderthal population grew smaller and they were pushed into the fringes of Spain. They should have disappeared ..."

"The way a computer vanishes when a new model comes along," the girl spoke up. Her eyes met Simon's and she smiled broadly. She might have been his age or maybe a year younger. Her hair was russet, she had the build of a gymnast, and her eyes were a beautiful coral colour. Like Emma and the others, she was very much the vrindh.

"Precisely," Michel said. "Forgive me. I haven't introduced Colleen, my daughter."

"Nice to meet you," Earl said. "I thought you were attending a school in Geneva. Did they let you out early?"

"No," the girl answered, with a faint French accent. "My father decided we should travel together. He picked me up yesterday and here we are."

"We haven't much time," Michel broke in nervously. "Let's get back to the subject at hand. As I was saying, the Neanderthals should have died out, but many of them didn't. Instead they developed an uncanny talent: their souls could leave their bodies and take animals over. A few could occupy trees and plants. And if a Cro-Magnon were weak or drunk or crazy, they could control him too. This talent enabled many to survive."

"But only in kaba form," Simon said. He was blushing slightly. Colleen was eyeing him still.

"Yes. Once they were living in vadhs and shatls, Cro-Magnon couldn't threaten them. But, as you say, this trick came at a price. They existed as spirits and little more." Michel charged a window on the far side of the room. He could hear a bird banging its wings against the pane. Inspecting the window more closely, he saw that the bird had built a nest outside. He smiled with relief. False alarm.

"What about the vrindhs?" Earl asked.

"They are different. Vrindhs come from bolkhs, or Neanderthals, who've survived in the flesh. We're mainly lura but part bolkh too. That means we can carry a bolkh's offspring. Our numbers are tiny but here we are."

"So what does Tarhlo want?" Simon asked. Colleen's eyes were on him still and he didn't know where to direct his gaze.

"He wants the bolkhs to flourish again. As spirits they can't reproduce — that's the price I mentioned. The only way they can regenerate is through …"

"Incarnation," Simon said.

"Yes. Incarnation. For generations they've plotted to return to the flesh. Once this is achieved, they can reproduce."

"In bodies like these?" Simon asked, motioning to the skeletons that, while shorter and stockier than the lura version, were graceful nonetheless.

"No. All such bodies have turned to dust, except for the vestiges that survive in us vrindhs. His plan is to take many luras over. By my estimate there are fifty thousand bolkhs at large. And many more are lying dormant in the forests of Europe. We're talking about a half million kabas — if all of them were incarnated, they could reproduce quickly. Within a hundred years they'd number in the tens of millions."

"But they can't occupy luras. So …"

"Your sister is the key. She is a hamax."

There was another disturbance outside. Earl walked over to investigate. Like Michel, he studied the bird's nest. His eyes narrowed in suspicion. It was normal enough but all four of them were worried.

"We shouldn't stay much longer," Earl said. "Let's wrap things up."

"The bolkhs have a tradition," Michel pressed on, speaking in a rush. "Once in a blue moon, a hamax can appear. This is a very rare occurrence and is marked by the appearance of twins, the hamax and her brother."

"What's so great about a hamax?"

"Take a look." Michel handed two more photographs over. These depicted more prehistoric scenes. In the first, a girl was carrying kabas inside her. They were smiling, as if the girl were a refuge. The second snapshot showed a man standing next to the girl. The painter had drawn a large circle above them, as though they were walking in some kind of bubble. A third photo contained a very different scene. It showed a ring of bolkhs with their hands joined together. They were circling a stag with a bolkh inside that was trying to escape its vadh, but couldn't quite manage.

As Earl handed the pictures back Michel spoke, "The drawings suggest that the hamax can carry multiple kabas, like a Noah's ark. If there's a shortage of vadhs, she'll keep the kabas from dying."

"Why would this be useful to Tarhlo?"

"I don't know. But he clearly has some plan in mind. The second photo shows that the woplh and hamax form a unit. I can't say what this means precisely, but your function, Simon, is to keep your sister safe. I also suspect you can bring out strengths in each other, that you're stronger together than you are alone." From habit, Michel glanced round nervously. "Finally, there's the third drawing. Its purpose is clear. When these bolkhs form a ring around a vadh, they can prevent its inner kaba from leaving. Like these gentlemen here."

He motioned to the skeletons that were standing in a ring and grinning like five jack-o'-lanterns, as if saying they would get the last laugh yet. The scene spooked everyone. It was time to go.

"Let's leave by different exits," Michel said, heading to a door at the room's north end. "As always, Earl, it has been a pleasure. And you, young man …"

"Yes?" Simon paused before the room's south exit.

"Tarhlo has something dreadful up his sleeve, and that's why I took my daughter from school. But perhaps you can stop him if you're true to your nature. Simply put, you must guard the hamax. No matter what, you must keep her safe. This is something only you can do. Best of luck and be very careful."

Colleen moved forward and took Simon's hand. "I hope we meet again," she said, before joining her father on the far side of the room. The pair of them exited, while Earl stepped past the southern door. Shaking off his torpor, Simon followed close behind.

As he left the stares from the skulls were burning holes in his back.

Chapter Sixteen

"How are you feeling?"

"A little better. The powder's maybe kicking in. The change of clothes is helping too. But I'm afraid I'm getting hungry again."

"Crispijn can pack the food away, can't he? But I'd rather not stop, if you don't mind. The sooner we reach the farm, the better I'll feel."

They were on the road and fifteen minutes away from the girls. After leaving the Natural History Museum, Earl had led them on a circuitous route through the crowded Latin Quarter and to the Île de la Cité. After milling in a huge crowd in Notre Dame Cathedral, they'd walked to a nearby Metro station and taken a train to the Châtelet, a hub packed with hordes of commuters who'd throw any lurking bolkh off their trail. From there they'd entered a department store, where they'd purchased Simon a new set of clothes as well as something to deal with his itching. Earl had proceeded to an underground lot, where he'd worked his usual magic and "borrowed" a car. After navigating the heart of city — they'd driven past the Louvre, the Place de la Concorde, the Champs Élysées, and Arc de Triomphe — they'd finally left the urban sprawl behind.

"If you really can't last," Earl went on, "there's a bag of pastry in my knapsack. It will take that pained look off your face."

"That's okay. I can wait," Simon replied.

To distract himself from the pangs in his stomach he decided to ask a difficult question. "Can you tell me something? You said earlier you didn't know about luras and bolkhs, not until my mother called. After that you were always running. How long did it take you to get used to the change?"

"Who says I got used to it?" Earl shot back. "How do you get used to something insane? I mean, souls that can control people if they're plastered? It's off the wall."

"Off the wall," Simon agreed.

"I'm still waiting to escape this nightmare. I keep thinking that I'll wake up in Toronto and Dolly will be brewing me coffee downstairs, as if I've been dreaming these last eighteen years. That tells you how much I'm used to this stuff."

"I'm scared," Simon admitted.

"I am too," he said.

They continued in silence for a few kilometres. It was late afternoon, the sun was hot, and the entire world seemed to be napping. The road was narrow and wound its way past many farms. Their progress was slow at times, when the occasional tractor blocked their path, hauling a wagon that was loaded with produce. There was livestock in the fields, but they were interested in grazing. The bolkhs weren't active in this neck of the woods. A boy was riding on a horse in the distance. He waved at Simon. Simon waved back.

A sign that read ALBERT, 20 KILOMETRES floated by.

"That was the site of a battle," Earl finally said. "During the First World War. Three hundred thousand men were killed. If you visit it today, the land is very pretty. The trenches are covered with grass and flowers, and people like to picnic there."

"You're telling me something."

"I guess. We've been fighting wars an awfully long time. They can be terrible, but the violence passes and peace breaks out. It doesn't last forever, true, but when you consider how our numbers have grown, peace generally outweighs the destruction."

"That sounds encouraging," Simon said. "But you don't sound cheerful."

"You're right," Earl agreed. "I have no idea where this struggle is leading. Humans are very good at war, when it's a matter of bombs, bullets, and missiles. But we've never fought any bolkhs before. As bad as things have been in the past, we've never faced a threat like this. That said …"

"Yeah?"

"I'm less scared now than I've been in ages. That's because of you. You give me courage, believe it or not. Just so you know."

Earl and Simon exchanged warm smiles. Then Earl signalled right and pulled into a lane that would lead them to their rented lodgings. The path took them up a hill that was overgrown with elms. When they'd climbed this incline the land flattened out, but the trees continued. The lane was black with shade. A kilometre beyond, in a sizeable clearing, the farmhouse beckoned. It looked solid, reliable, safe, and cozy.

Except the elms were suddenly laden with birds. Some branches were so thick with crows, starlings, sparrows, and other species that they were bending under the weight. There were hundreds of these creatures, thousands even, and all were watching the car advance. There wasn't a sound. Not a single peep.

That wasn't true. Just then, Earl's cellphone rang. With a look of panic, Simon answered.

"Dis is a moment of crisis," a voice spoke mockingly. "You hear me? A moment of crisis!" Simon felt his heart stop when he grasped that it was Cletho speaking. He hung up the phone.

"So they've found us," Earl said matter-of-factly. "All along they knew where we were."

"What do we do now?"

"We see what they want."

Shifting to a low gear, he moved forward at a crawl. As soon as he left the trees for the clearing, the birds took wing in one large mass. It was as if a veil was hiding the sun. A pall of shadows encompassed them and escorted the car as it inched its way forward. In the fields flanking both sides of the road, dogs, cats, and livestock appeared. The dogs stood still and stared at Simon with a yearning that made Crispijn's blood freeze over. When they stopped in a driveway in front of the house, eight figures lumbered out. Two were women, six were males, but all were hollow-eyed and violent looking.

There was no sign of the girls.

"No matter what happens," Earl said, coming to a stop and applying the hand-brake, "it's up to you. If they tie me up or do something worse, you have to keep going and rescue your sister. You can't afford to fail. Do you understand?"

"Where is she? And what about Emma and Jenny?"

"Pay attention! You must save Clara. Is that clear?"

"I can't see them …"

"Listen! This battle isn't over unless you surrender. You have to keep pushing, no matter what! Is that clear?"

Simon exchanged looks with his uncle. Earl was nervous but his determination shone through. If he could keep his head when threatened like this, how could Simon not follow his example?"

"It's clear," he said, squeezing Earl hard. "I'll fight to the finish. I won't give in, no matter what."

"Good," Earl said, with the thinnest of smiles. "That's all anyone can ask of you. Okay, let's not keep our hosts waiting any longer."

He undid his seat belt and left the car. Simon did the same. As soon as they were outside, the figures closed in. They were smiling vacantly and clawing the air in their anxiety to work the pair of them over.

"*Leave 'em be!*" an enormous crow cried out, settling in front of them. Cletho. "*Dose are Tarhlo's orders! Y'unnderstand?*

"*Well, well,*" he continued, "*if it ain't Simon Carpenter. Though by now you know you ain't him at all.*"

"I'm glad you escaped that hamster," Simon said, with a look that suggested he was almost bored. "But where's Clara hiding? And what about my mother and cousin?"

"*You'll find out soon.*" Cletho cackled. "*But your uncle don't get bolkhin 'n looks confused. Hang on a sec while I switch into a shatl.*"

A moment later a burly man with a tangled beard stepped forward. His skull was shaved and scarred all over, a sign that surgeons had cut into his brain. Simon watched as the guy was suddenly filled with understanding, the result of Cletho having taken him over.

The bolkh resumed speaking, only this time as a human. "Dat's better. So dis is the famous Earl? You must be quite a guy, to have escaped Tarhlo for eighteen years. But we finally caught you, Mr. Smarty Pants."

"You got lucky," Earl drawled.

"It warn't luck, buster," Cletho said with a smirk. "We've been trackin' you since yesterday. We knew where you were holin' up but decided to wait 'till we collected de right muscle. Can you guess how we was keepin' tabs?"

Earl shook his head.

"T'roo him," Cletho said, motioning to Simon. "You know how you stopped when dat truck was all smashed? Dat warn't no accident, no sirree. I steered dat pig into de truck, knowin' it would crash 'n you'd try pushin' it outta de way. 'N when Simon neared de pig, t'ree of our Khalkons infected him. Dey's were in de lice infestin' de sow 'n it warn't no problem to fly demselves over. Dese bolkhs have been givin' us de goods 'bout your location, see?"

Simon cringed in disgust. Crispijn had lice? So that explained his itchiness, not to mention how the bolkhs had tracked them down. He cursed in silence. How could they prevail against an enemy like this?

"Very clever," Earl said, utterly unfazed. "So what's the plan? Are your goons going to murder me, the way your boss killed my wife? She was his cousin, in case you didn't know."

"She was a lura lover!" Cletho yelled with naked contempt. But his voice softened instantly, "But 'tings have changed 'n you don't gotta worry. We ain't gonna lay a finger on you. I'stead, you'll stay here under de eye of my colleagues."

"You're joking," Earl answered.

"No kiddin', buster. Tarhlo knows dat victory's near. As de uncle of the hamax, you deserve some respect. So you'll sit tight here until we unite youse wid your sister."

"Where is my sister? And what about my daughter?"

"Dey is safe and no concern o' yours. But dat's enuff from you. Take him off."

The goons grabbed Earl and led him away. They weren't all that gentle, but they weren't rough either. Simon watched him leave with regret. It was easier to feel courage when a friend was near. Still, he remembered his vow to Earl and suppressed a mounting wave of despair.

"What about me?" he asked, in the same calm tone as his uncle's.

"Dat's easy," Cletho said. "It's time fer you to meet your dad. Your real dad and not dat ridiculous lura."

"Is he here?"

"Here?" Cletho sneered. "Why would he be here? He's leading Clara, or Kralha, to the *domh*, togedder wid de udders. Dat's where we'll be meetin' him."

"The *domh*?"

"You's really are ignorant, ain't you? De domh's de very last home we had. It's in a place de luras now call Gibraltar. Tarhlo figgers it's de place to launch our invasion. Poetic justice, if youse get my meanin'. Still, 'nuff o' dat. We's got a lotta sky to cover 'n jawin' on ain't goin' to get it done. Let's get movin'.'"

Cletho beckoned to the flock around them. Instantly a bird flew near and stood in front of Simon. It was a common swallow, with a yellow breast and dark blue wings. It was small and unimpressive looking, but strong and capable of long-distance travel.

"Leave de lug 'n get i'side de bird. And I mean pronto."

"What about Crispijn?"

"He ain't your concern no longer. Take de bird over. Now!"

With a sigh, Simon did as he was told. Bidding Crispijn's kaba farewell — it was still turning feebly in circles — he quit the body and jumped into the swallow, brushing by the bolkh that was leaving it behind. It was like picking up a car from a valet, he imagined.

"*Dat's better.*" Cletho spoke from a second swallow. "*Let's get started. De sooner we leave, de sooner we arrive.*"

No sooner had he finished speaking than the mass of birds took flight, swallows, crows, starlings, thrushes, and a dozen other local species. Simon was near the head of them, with Cletho by his side. As the flock spiralled higher and higher, Simon watched the farmhouse and Crispijn grow smaller.

His hopes were shrinking just as quickly.

Chapter Seventeen

The sun was peeping over the horizon, casting a pale light over the water. The sea was in a tranquil mood and breaking playfully against the shore, depositing seashells and strands of seaweed. To Simon's right lay the Mediterranean. To his left, miles distant, was the bruising Atlantic. Immediately below was a huge mass of stone, much of which was covered in gorse.

Two nights had passed since they'd left the farm-house, and in that time the flock had covered lots of ground. Winging past Paris — Simon had spied the Eiffel Tower — they'd flown due south over a landscape of fields, forests, vineyards, towns, factories, rivers, lakes, and multiple highways. In Bordeaux they'd found fresh birds to fly in and travelled through the night, across the Pyrenees and into Spain. At dawn they'd stopped in Zaragoza and rustled up another contingent of birds — Simon had taken over a gull. They'd headed south again and reached the heart of Madrid. As the sun was setting they alighted in Seville. Switching birds one final time, the bolkhs had journeyed through the night to Cadiz, where, floating in a golden halo, a mosque and a cathedral stood side by side. After witnessing a second dawn, they were approaching a cave on the coast of Gibraltar.

They descended swiftly, a wave of heat rising up from the soil to greet them. The currents here were tricky and threatened to grab them and toss them out to sea. With a concerted burst of energy, and with Cletho in the lead, they just managed to conquer the winds and alight upon a series of rocks. A cave entrance lay a few metres away, but the group was too exhausted to pay it any notice. They needed time to catch their breath.

There was no rest for Simon.

A boy approached. He was eight, slim, and his eyes were badly swollen, as if he'd taken a terrible beating. To judge by his complexion and sharp-cut features, Simon guessed his shatl had been snatched in Morocco, a dozen miles south of Gibraltar.

"Where is the woplh?" he demanded, in a high-pitched voice.

"Over here," Cletho screeched from inside a whiskered tern. He used a wing to point at Simon.

"I am Darthlo. Follow me," the boy told Simon, as he ducked inside the cave.

Simon and Cletho followed close behind. They waddled a few metres into the cave and then stopped before a towering shelf of rock. Simon tried to gauge the cave's depth, but the hollows in front of him were steeped in shadow. As far as he could tell, they ran on forever.

Darthlo pointed to the shelf without saying a word. Sprawled across it was a young boy's body that looked exactly like Darthlo's shatl, the difference being this kid was sleeping. A breeze from the sea stirred his tight black curls.

"Take him over," Darthlo ordered Simon.

"You heard him," Cletho prodded.

Simon broke loose of the gull he'd been riding, approached the body, and plunged inside. Settling in and seizing the controls, he wriggled the fingers and flexed the arms. The eyes didn't respond at first but by focusing hard he got them to work.

"Wow," Darthlo spoke.

"Wow's right," Cletho said, without his usual scorn.

Simon wondered what the big deal was. They still didn't know that he'd mastered projection? Hadn't Cletho seen him ride a series of vadhs and …

Then he understood. The shatl's kaba wasn't drunk or damaged or sleeping. It was stone-cold dead. It was sprawled out just below the liver and betrayed no glow or the slightest sign of motion.

He'd taken over a corpse.

Panic struck. He lost his grip. The limbs started wilting and the boy dropped to his knees. Aware that Simon wanted to bolt, Cletho flew at him and beat him with his wings.

"*Stay dere!*" he screeched. "*Dose are Tarhlo's orders! Dere's nothin' wrong wid de shatl you're in. So de kaba ain't alive — big deal.*"

"Why have you forced me into a corpse?" Simon

asked. He could hardly get these syllables out because to do so he had to use the dead boy's tongue.

"It's a test," a voice boomed out. "Only Tarhlo's son could project into a corpse. This is a gift that only Khalkon leaders possess. I am pleased to say that you have passed with flying colours and proven you truly are Krahl Tarhlo-tal."

The voice was coming from inside the cave. Simon stared into the darkness then scrambled to his feet as someone emerged. The cave was maybe two metres high, yet this shatl's head was almost grazing the ceiling. This person it belonged to also came from Morocco: the skin was dark, the build slender, and the eyes black and burning bright. It was dressed in a pale white burnoose and moved with the grace and grandeur of a king.

"Are you Tarhlo?" Simon asked.

"I am your father," Tarhlo answered. "For sixteen years we've been kept apart. I can't tell you how much I have yearned for this day."

"And Emma, Clara, and Jenny? Where are they? You haven't hurt them?"

"I will take you to them shortly. And why would I hurt them? Emma is my wife. Clara is my blood. I would lay my kaba down to protect them."

"That's because you need them in your war against the luras. That's your plan, isn't it? To destroy the luras?"

Cletho squawked and Darthlo gasped in horror. Bolkhs didn't address their leader in this fashion, not if they wished to keep their kaba intact. And sure enough, Tarhlo glared at Simon fiercely, as if intent on punishing this show of defiance. Just as quickly his features softened and he smiled widely. His sudden radiance was as warm as the sun outside.

"You have been raised by luras all your life," he said, chuckling, "yet still your Khalkon temper shines through. That makes my heart glow. Come with me. I will explain everything."

He strode toward the mouth of the cave, moving smoothly and with perfect balance. They soon emerged on a stretch of rock that was drenched in light from the mounting sun. Striding past the hemindhs who'd escorted Simon, Tarhlo started on an upward path.

They climbed without speaking for the next fifteen minutes. The path was steep and required all their breath. The rocks and vegetation scratched their limbs and both were gasping and pouring sweat — Simon could taste blood at the back of his throat. His shatl didn't like being pushed this hard. "I'm dead," it seemed to say as he forced it upward. They continued without resting until Tarhlo surmounted a crest of rock from which the length and breadth of Gibraltar could be seen.

"Look," Tarhlo panted, slick with perspiration. "We stand before two continents. There is Africa," he said, motioning south, "and Europe beckons over there." He pointed north.

Simon was dazzled. The entire world was on display, with vast lands unfolding to the north and south, and with the Atlantic and Mediterranean to his right and left. The sun was smiling and seemed to be saying, "Now you know what I see every day."

"This northern land?" Tarhlo continued, opening his arms as if to embrace it. "It was ours. All of it belonged to the bolkhs. For ten thousand generations we were masters of its soil. All its beasts were ours to hunt, we fished its lakes and picked its fruits, helping ourselves as we saw fit. The rain and snow could treat us with disdain, but we cowered before no living creature."

He considered Simon. Tarhlo's expression was serene. With a start, Simon realized that he was witnessing greatness. Never mind that Tarhlo was a force of destruction. Simon sensed his authoritative will.

There was a disturbance in the sky. An eagle was in hot pursuit of a dove. The dove was trying hard to escape, flapping frantically and twisting left and right, to no avail. Almost playfully the eagle stayed on its tail, turning when it turned and keeping up with ease. As the dove approached a face of rock and the lure of safety, the eagle swiftly ended the charade. With a burst of speed, it collided with the dove and, shooting out its talons, ripped its jugular apart. With a shriek of satisfaction, it carried the dove off.

The sight caused Tarhlo to glower.

"Then they came," he spoke, motioning south. "The luras left Africa, strayed across our boundaries, and hunted what was ours. In the beginning we outnumbered them, a hundred to one. Over time, their size, their streamlined weapons, their cunning, speed, and overall wisdom raised them above us, high above us, and made them more successful than us. Our spoils became theirs. They fed better than we did and produced more children, season after season. Occasionally we fought and again they proved superior. Over time their numbers grew larger than ours. Bit by bit we retreated south. That land you travelled past when you flew from Paris? It belonged to us. The fields, forests, rivers, and lakes, once upon a time we controlled them all. But the luras took them. They took everything over. Even this rock, our very last preserve, they seized it too. In their arrogance and greed, they left us nothing. They watched us die without lifting a finger!"

Tarhlo's rage was too terrible to contain. He emitted a bloodcurdling scream. The sound bounced across the rock and echoed out to sea. His mouth was open, his teeth were bared, and his eyes were wide with rage and sorrow — Simon thought of the skulls in the Natural History Museum.

Tarhlo regained control. Inhaling deeply, he pressed on. "I shouldn't be angry. It was nature's doing that we were beaten. That dove we saw the eagle destroy? Its wings are shorter, its beak is weak, and its talons are blunt and have no power. Nature made it so and that is why the eagle prevails. The same harsh reality applied to us. The luras were taller, wiser, stronger. Victory was justly theirs. But now *we* are favoured. *We* will outlast them. *We* will be incarnated and *they* will perish. It is sad that nature delights in competition, but we can't be blamed if, like all living kabas, we fight and destroy to protect our own."

Tarhlo seized Simon and drew him in close. Simon's face was so near to his father's that their noses were touching and Tarhlo's breath was hot against his skin. Looking straight into his eyes, Simon spied his father's kaba and almost reeled at the sight of the emotions it bared: longing, sorrow, humiliation, heartbreak, and, above all else, white-hot fury.

"Do you understand why I plot?" he murmured. "Perhaps you think I am violent and unjust. But survival *is* justice. Triumph *is* justice. Revenge *is* justice. If you measure me by nature's rule, you will find that I am no less just than the passing seasons."

He released his son and drew himself straight. Facing north, and moving off from Simon, he spoke in a tone that was threatening and tender. "I do not blame your mother for leaving and seeking refuge with the lura family. And I do not blame you for your feelings of confusion — these last few days your world has been upended. But you can't return to the lura world. The family that nurtured you has their real son back. Your blood is different and you have no place among them. If they invited you over, in what body would you visit? What would you discuss? What future would you share? No, you are a bolkh, pure and simple. The sooner you accept this truth, the sooner you'll fulfill the role that nature has devised for you."

Without another word, Tarhlo started down the path. While his abrupt departure took Simon by surprise, he understood his father's message: the time for speech was over and action counted now.

Simon considered the view. The air was still and the light was soft and golden. If anything, he was more confused than ever. Tarhlo's words had stirred him deeply and turned his thinking inside out. His father — his father! — wasn't a vicious killer, as he'd been thinking since he'd spied him at Koblansky's. He was looking after his people's interests. When the bolkhs recorded their history, he would be their Abraham Lincoln.

All this begged a difficult question. Whose side was Simon on?

"This day has been a thousand lifetimes in the making. In that time our enemy has enslaved the land, built cities, launched wars, created machines, and lorded over the skies. All of this, everything, has come at our expense. Their well-being has been a product of our exile. But this day, this moment, will redress the balance. From this day forward we will be incarnated. And once we are made flesh again, we will increase our numbers and spread our tribes across the soil!"

Tarhlo paused and a clamour arose. Five thousand creatures expressed cries of approval, birds, cats, dogs, sheep, goats, and others. They were gathered in the domh — a hollow at the core of the Rock of Gibraltar. It was large enough to put a stadium to shame and had a ceiling as high as St. Peter's in Rome — it also bristled with stalactites that resembled teeth on an ogre.

The cavern's strangest feature was the slabs at its centre. They had somehow fallen atop each other — unless they'd been dragged by the bolkhs themselves — to form a giant table-like structure. Tarhlo was addressing

Nicholas Maes

the crowd from this surface, like a priest addressing a church congregation.

The "table" impressed Simon for another reason. When he'd visited Clara back in Vancouver, he remembered her showing him a series of drawings. One had featured this very table, as if she'd known even then that events would lead them here.

Clara. She was standing next to Tarhlo and staring blankly at the crowd. An hour earlier she'd consumed a dark concoction. Within seconds she had fallen into a stupor and Tarhlo had led her to the tabletop, with Jenny and Emma poised close by. Clara looked helpless on the stone formation, especially since the crowd was eyeing her so ravenously. They were squirming with excitement and awaiting the signal to proceed.

"Some have complained that our triumph will be slow, that it will take at least three generations. In response I say the wait will be easy. After those three generations we will have power again. It took ten thousand winters for the luras to destroy us. Fifty winters later we will far surpass the luras. You must be patient, all of you, as we join our spears together and bring our quarry to bay. Then we will chant around the fire:

> Sun glows always
> Moon glows always
> Stars glow always
> They have no children.
> Their eyes are clear,
> Their hands are clean,

Their minds are pure,
They have no children.
We glow and die
Our hands are stained
Our minds are cruel
But we have children.
And they will bleed
And they will die
And they will kill
To have their children.

The crowd was swaying. To Simon's surprise, he was swaying too. From the table Tarhlo caught his eye and grinned, as if to say, "You see? You do belong here." His smile faded. The moment had come.

"But let us stall no longer. Defeat is behind us. In the distance stands a meadow of gold. Between this meadow and our triumph flows a river of blood. Who will wade through this to the lands that beckon? Who among the Khalkons, Stemhlons, Mastavars, Troglads Threedhs, and Khastrins will join their spears to mine and battle wind and rain and snow? Who is tired of meatless seasons? Who hates the fire that denies him warmth? Who craves water that will slake his thirst? Up, brothers! Up, sisters! Leave this barren flesh behind and enter our hamax, the engine of deliverance!"

He bellowed like a bull. This must have been a signal. There were barks, cheeps, mews, and growls as thousands of kabas abandoned their vessels. A wind-like roar blew across the cavern, as if a storm had been unleashed, and Tarhlo kept bellowing and howling with laughter.

Even as the bolkhs left their vessels behind, Tarhlo's henchmen herded them to the mouth of the cave, although the task wasn't easy. The tumult in the chamber was overwhelming.

Simon kept his eyes on Clara. Her mouth was open, her nostrils flared. Her limbs were shaking spastically now, as if she were being riddled with bullets or stung by a million bees at once. Several times she jumped clear of the ground and her head twisted at an ugly angle. She was trying to scream but no sound would escape. She also tried to shield herself, but her hands and feet weren't hers to control.

Simon tried to move in close, to help her through this torture. But as he strained against the shatls about him, Tarhlo nodded to the hemindhs, who cut him off.

And then it stopped. Clara's limbs were still, her eyes were closed, and her features were composed, unnaturally so. Jenny and Emma looked terrified but Tarhlo was beaming. And why not? Over five thousand bolkhs were packed inside his daughter.

Simon was half-sick with fear. Clara looked pale and tiny in that cavern. How ironic, then, that she was deadlier by far than all the armies in the world combined.

The luras wouldn't even know what hit them.

They were walking single file down a path. Their goal was a car on the road below. Tarhlo went first — he was guiding Clara. Behind her were Emma and Jenny, who were trailed by Simon and a number of goons. Simon had tried to stand next to Clara but Tarhlo and his agents had intervened. Cletho was bringing up the rear. They'd been walking for twenty minutes and the path was flattening out.

While the bolkhs were cheerful and joking with each other, Simon and the girls were down in the mouth. Clara was drugged and oblivious to everything, Emma was too frightened to speak, and Jenny was her taciturn self. They hadn't said anything since they'd started on this walk. That's why Simon was surprised when Jenny turned and murmured softly, "Remember: follow in my wake."

"What?"

"You've seen my kaba. You can read it. Remember to do so."

Simon wanted her to explain more fully but they'd reached the road. The goons were all over them and they couldn't speak freely. A minute later they were beside the car. When Simon tried to approach Clara, Tarhlo cut him off.

"Let us drink before we leave," he said, unstringing a leather skin from his shoulder. Cletho pulled wooden cups from his knapsack. Filling these with the drink that Clara had swallowed, Tarhlo passed the cups around, setting one in Simon's hand. He left out Jenny and Emma, however.

"May our efforts prove successful," he said, raising his cup and glancing the group over, "and may every hunter receive his dues."

Crying *"Stolh!"* they drank with grunts of satisfaction.

"Please don't take it hard, Son," Tarhlo said, eyeing Simon warmly. "You are with us but your spear has no place in this hunt."

"What?" Simon answered. He was about to press Tarhlo to explain. Before he could, the earth seemed to wobble, Tarhlo grew distant, and a cloud of blackness descended.

His last conscious thought was, "I've failed my sister."

Chapter Eighteen

"How do you feel?"

"Groggy."

"Course you do. *Smakho*'s strong. I'm amazed you've only been out for sixteen hours. On tastin' it de first time, most bolkhs don't recover for at least a week. Dey're a lot like zombies 'n can be steered wherever. It also plays wid deir power to project."

"That's why Tarhlo gave it to my sister?"

"You've got dat right."

Simon's head was killing him — or rather, the head that belonged to his corpse of a shatl. He was lying in the cavern. The goons had carried him back from the car as soon as Tarhlo and the girls had left. He could hear the hemindhs laughing in the background and joking about what the future would bring. Cletho had opted to sit beside Simon — his shatl was bald and had a stump for a hand. He was friendlier than normal. This was partly because Simon was Tarhlo's son and the hamax's brother, and partly because he was drunk on smakho.

"Drink some of dis," he said, handing Simon a cloudy liquid. "It's great at counteractin' smakho."

"What is it?" Simon asked with suspicion, staring down into the wooden cup. "It sure smells funny."

"It's milk, oregano, and thyme," Cletho said. "Go on, drink. It ain't poison, believe me."

"That does feel better," Simon admitted after taking a sip. "Thanks."

"Sure."

"So what's going on?"

"What's goin' on?" Cletho asked, in a deadpan tone that concealed his excitement. "Let's see. Oh yeah, we're incarnatin' bolkhs."

"Yeah, I know. But how exactly?"

Cletho eyed him doubtfully. To judge by his expression, he'd been warned to keep things secret; on the other hand, the smakho had him wanting to blab. In the end, his drunkenness beat his prudence out.

"Your sister's a hamax. You know what dat means?"

"Sure."

"And we wanna be incarnated."

"Yeah. So?"

"So figure it out. You know what limnls are, don't you?"

"I should. I was one myself. But I still don't get it. Unless …"

Simon's jaw dropped. A possibility struck home, so simple, so obvious, yet so horribly ruthless. Tarhlo wouldn't. He couldn't.

"Dat's right," Cletho said, with a burst of laughter. "I can tell by your puss dat you've pieced it togedder. De plan is to find babies dat've just been delivered. Tarhlo'll lead your sister to dem and de bolkhs i'side her'll push de newborn kabas out. Dat'll produce five t'ousand limnls lickitysplit."

"Wow. But where can he find newborns clustered together?"

"In maternity wards, dat's where," Cletho crowed, as if he'd come up with this plan himself. "He's gonna travel from one ward to de next, chasing out lura kabas just when dey've appeared. In de past, bolkhs found newborns by luck — dat's why limnls are incredibly rare. 'N if we entered a ward in our usual shatls, drunks 'n udder lakhn types, we'd be tossed on our keisters. But wid a hamax, we can sneak in by de hundreds, de t'ousands, 'n no nurse ain't gonna t'row a l'il girl from de ward."

"It's ingenious. Where are these wards?"

"Wouldn't you like to know? I'll give you a hint. Dey ain't nearby. Tarhlo's flown to a place where de pickin's are rich. More t'an dat, I can't tell you."

Cletho added that this was just the beginning. There were hundreds of thousands of bolkhs worldwide. After Clara launched the initial group — that would take at least a couple of weeks — she would return to Gibraltar and load up again. After eighteen months, every bolkh would be a limnl. And with hundreds of thousands of limnls at large, the seeds would be sown for huge numbers to follow.

As Cletho spoke Simon had to stop himself from retching. He'd known all along that Tarhlo's plan would be violent, but he'd never guessed his victims would be newborns. How could anyone target a baby? Even if Simon agreed that the bolkhs had suffered, and that the luras had to pay somehow, why should newborns die by the thousands?

Tarhlo would argue that this was war. Had the luras shown pity for the bolkhs long ago? Hadn't they been just as cruel and indifferent? Hadn't bolkh babies died in horrifying numbers? If the bolkhs could only win by destroying newborns then the deaths were justified, necessary even. In a fight for survival there was no right and wrong.

And Tarhlo wouldn't stop there. He would remind his son of his place with them, that his days of living with the luras were over, and that the Carpenters would never want to see him again, especially if he visited in the guise of a corpse. He'd been born a bolkh and he would die one too. And the same line of reasoning applied to Clara ...

Clara. The thought of his sister brought him up short. *She'd* warned Emma that Tarhlo was dangerous, *she'd* caused Emma to flee to Vancouver, and *she'd* preferred that home to living with her father. Why? Because Tarhlo's schemes disgusted her. From birth she'd known what he was up to, how central her own role would be, and still she'd rejected Tarhlo's ambitions. Maybe survival wasn't such a big deal, not if innocents had to pay the price.

His choice seemed clear. As a woplh, he was supposed to follow his sister. If her instincts said this scheme was wrong, who was he to question her judgement? He would join her side, his uncle's too. If this meant living apart from bolkhs and luras, then this would be the price he'd pay.

"… Arithmetic ain't my strength," Cletho said, drowsy from the smakho, "but we bolkhs have a lot of kids, twenty on average — least we did when we could reproduce. If you factor dis in over fifty years, startin' with two hundred t'ousand parents, our tribes'll grow even faster dan rabbits. So it ain't ridiculous to hope dat we'll take over one day."

"If this plan is so glorious," Simon asked, "how come Tarhlo didn't take us along? You're his assistant and I'm the woplh."

"I'm arrangin' de next crowd o' kabas," Cletho yawned. "And it's 'cause you're de woplh dat he don't want you wid 'em. You might interfere 'cause you ain't never hunted. Not bein' used to killin', your heart is soft. And to mix de hamax 'n you togedder, well, dat ain't exactly a good ideer."

"So I'm your prisoner?"

"Our prisoner?" Cletho laughed. "You're a Khalkon 'n a woplh! Like we could hold you if you t'ought of escapin'! Dat's rich!"

"So I can leave?"

"Any time! Who's gonna stop you? But if you were plottin' to interfere, it ain't gonna happen. You don't know Tarhlo's where'bouts so dere ain't no catchin' up wid him!" He screeched with laughter. After a minute his laughter turned to chuckles, then his chuckles to grunts, and his grunts to snores. Pretty soon he was out for the count.

Nicholas Maes

Simon sighed and asked himself the question again. Bolkhs or luras? He pictured Clara being blasted with kabas and imagined this crowd hurting lura newborns. No question about it. His loyalties were clear.

Without wasting time, he took off from his shatl. There was an indecent sound as air left the throat and the vessel became Death's possession again. Simon felt bad about killing the flesh, but the boy was dead and his fate was sealed already. Besides, those newborns were counting on him.

Spying a beetle, he jumped inside it. He spread its wings and gradually stole from the cave. Cletho's snores were echoing through its hollows. They seemed to jeer at him that he was backing the wrong team and his efforts would end in disappointment.

From deep inside a kingfisher, Simon was surveying Gibraltar from a dizzying height. After the cave, the sun was glorious to bask in. It was close to noon, as far as he could tell. For the fifteenth time he studied the land closely. Its main spur looked unfriendly, but its villas and swimming pools gave it charm. There were several ships at sea, freighters, speedboats, and fishing vessels, and each leaving a wake behind it. Everything looked normal, which bothered Simon. How could things look normal when Tarhlo was plotting his bolkh revolution?

As he flitted about the peninsula, Simon wondered what his next step was. He had to find Clara, but how? Cletho had given him nothing to go on, except that

Tarhlo was where the pickings were rich. Because Emma and Jenny weren't able to project, and Clara clearly needed her shatl, they'd be forced to travel by normal means — a car, a boat, or a plane, most likely. So their first stop would have been the airport, maybe.

The airport. It was directly below, on the neck of land joining Gibraltar to Europe. A jet was taking off just then, but where was it headed? There were dozens of possible destinations. If Simon was right and they were travelling by plane, there was no predicting what the target was — Africa, Asia, Europe, the Americas. So how could Simon track them down?

He cheeped in frustration as he circled the Rock. Just as he was thinking that he should return to the cave and try to shake an answer from Cletho, never mind that the bolkh was unlikely to crack, he happened to scan the water again. The boats looked so elegant and yet something about them was teasing his brain. What? Each of them was different, from the freighters to the fishing crafts, so …

The wake! That was it! Each was trailing a wake. What had Jenny murmured when they were hiking down the hill? "Follow in my wake." What did she mean? What was her wake? Was it linked to that stunt over at the farmhouse, when she'd persuaded him to jump at her so he'd recognize her feel? He mulled this over. There was one way to find out.

He steered his vadh toward the airport.

—/—/—

Simon was in a lizard. He was watching the departures hall, which was spacious but nothing like the one in Vancouver. It was fifty metres long and five metres tall. There were a dozen airline counters, a snack bar, and some shops. He'd searched them all for a clue from Jenny but nothing had jumped out at him. His legs were tired from running all over and his desperation was fast returning.

A woman walked by and almost crushed him with her heels. Dodging behind the leg of a chair, he saw her approach the women's washroom. The washroom! It was the one place left that he hadn't checked, because he was making lura assumptions and believed such places were off-limits to him. But he was a lizard now and couldn't afford to be squeamish. Running at full tilt, he zipped past the door as the woman in the heels wheeled it open.

His plan was to inspect each of the stalls, but that proved unnecessary. Over by the sinks, in the floor's far corner, a familiar waft caught his interest. He slipped across the tiles to sniff things out.

His goal was a wad of dried out spit. As disgusting as that was — though in lizard form it wasn't terrible — it conveyed Jenny's aura to Simon's senses. Why, he couldn't say. His kaba's "antennae" just told him so. That had to mean the spit was hers. But there was something else. Beneath the spit? Letters had been scrawled, in ballpoint pen. "NYC-JFK" they read — shorthand for New York City, JFK International Airport.

He experienced a thrill. His entire lizard's body shook. Jenny assumed that Simon was tracking her and would leave more clues as he followed her trail.

He didn't waste a second. Exiting the washroom when the door next opened, he sped toward the electronic screens. Because he couldn't see them from his lizard's perspective, he left this vadh and studied them in kaba form.

There! A flight for JFK was listed. It was leaving from Gate 6 in … seven minutes. Panic-stricken, he searched for his lizard: free to wander, it had up and vanished. But there was a movement by the window, on the far side of the hall. Darting over, Simon stumbled on a ladybug.

Hijacking this vadh, Simon steered it toward the gates and passed security with the greatest of ease. A minute later he was nearing Gate 6. An agent was processing the final passenger, a distinguished-looking man in a pinstriped suit. He was greying at the temples and carrying a briefcase. As the woman handed him his boarding pass, Simon perched himself on the guy's left shoulder. Blind to his presence, the man boarded the bus that would take him over the tarmac to a 747. Feeling exposed, Simon hid under his lapel.

The only thing lacking was a seat belt, he mused.

Chapter Nineteen

Simon was on the man's shoulder and looking around. They were standing in the arrivals hall at JFK and Simon's ride was waiting for his luggage to show. A crowd had gathered at the baggage carousel but only a dozen bags had come out. People were cursing, kids were going crazy, and a terrier in a cage was howling away.

Simon was thinking: Tarhlo had arrived yesterday at roughly the same time, 8:30 p.m. Even if they'd spent the entire night sleeping, he and the girls would have been busy that day. How many newborns had they ousted so far? Fifty? A hundred? Two hundred? More? Maternity wards were open twenty-four/seven and by pumping Clara full of smakho, Tarhlo could keep her working around the clock.

He had to find his sister.

A woman had freed the terrier and was stroking his ears. It had fallen silent and was settling down. Except that it suddenly leapt from its owner, jumped to the tiles, and dashed into the crowd. As he steered the animal past a forest of legs, Simon heard the woman screaming, "Petey! Baby! Where're you going?"

The first washroom he checked had nothing to offer. No trace of Jenny hung in the air. Threading the terrier past another wall of people, Simon lunged into a second washroom, but again it proved fruitless. By then the authorities were on his tail. Three figures in suits were running toward him, yelling commands into their walkie-talkies. From far away the woman was screeching, "Petey! Come back! Don't hurt my baby!"

Reaching the third women's washroom was hard. Petey had six guards on his tail and various bystanders were trying to grab him. Twice he was missed by inches, and the shouts and laughter were very distracting. The little dog wasn't used to such running and its heart was pounding like crazy. Just when he was sure the mutt would collapse, Simon spied the third washroom and dashed inside it.

They were faint but he picked up traces of Jenny. He searched the corners, the pipes beneath the sinks, and the turquoise tiles behind the two garbage cans. Three uniformed women entered the room. He inspected the stalls, one by one. He got lucky in the fourth one. In the join between the wall and toilet there was a gob of spit and letters in red ink: "St. Luke's Roosevelt Mat. Ward. Manhat."

Aha!

"Got you!" a woman yelled, grabbing Petey and holding him tight. The terrier was spent and barely moved a muscle. A minute later it was back with its owner, who was crying hysterically and wailing over and over, "My baby! My baby!" Simon was about to leave poor Petey and find a way to get to St. Luke's, when the woman told the dog, "You'll feel better when you see Central Park from our window. Would you like that, sweetie?"

Simon had never been to New York, but he knew from the movies and various books that Central Park was in Manhattan.

"Give me two more hours," he told the dog's kaba, *"then you'll never have to see me again."*

The dog whined, as if to say, *"You've got a deal."*

From inside Petey, Simon gasped as they emerged from the Midtown Tunnel. The lights of Manhattan were spread before them, along with buildings of every size and description, a weight of masonry so impossibly huge that it was a miracle the island didn't buckle and sink. It was almost 10:00 p.m. yet the bars were full, pedestrians were everywhere, and the traffic was ridiculous. Simon had thought Paris was large, but Manhattan put its dimensions to shame.

As he revelled in the chaos, he grasped why Tarhlo had come to New York City. It was overcrowded and its mat wards would be packed. If he wanted newborns in high concentrations, this sprawling metropolis was the right place to be. Simon had to give it to him — the guy was clever.

He figured there was no sense staying in Petey. They were heading north as far as he could tell. They were speeding past the UN Plaza, which he recognized from his dad's favourite movie, *North by Northwest*. Because the cab was maybe driving away from St. Luke's his best bet was to abandon the dog and find a shatl that could steer him straight.

That didn't take long. At East 47th Street he spied a man lying on a concrete wall. His tie was crooked, his hair uncombed, and he was out of place in those fancy surroundings. He was singing too. He had to be drunk. Simon bade Petey farewell and left the cab through a half-open window.

"*Who are you?*" the guy's kaba yelled as Simon wrested control of his limbs. He could tell the guy had eaten garlic for dinner and the aching knuckles on his right hand revealed that he'd been fighting.

"*Where's St. Luke's Roosevelt?*" Simon asked.

"*At least introduce yourself!*" the kaba cried indignantly. "*What are you? An alien or something?*"

"*My name's Simon, if you really want to know. So where's St. Luke's Hospital?*"

"*Is your wife having a baby, mack?*"

"*Something like that,*" Simon answered.

"*Why didn't you say so? Okay, here's what you do: go due north to 58th. You taking a cab?*"

"*I'll be travelling by bird.*"

"*No kidding? Head west on 58th, fly over Central Park, pass Columbus Circle until you reach 10th Avenue. If you like Greek food, there's this joint on 4th …*"

But Simon had already left the man, whom he half-admired for his friendliness and gumption. New Yorkers. Go figure.

Halfway down the block, on a building's ledge, he discovered a flock of pigeons roosting. He nabbed one and used it to fly straight up a hundred storeys, then he headed north. A wealth of noise and lights assailed him. Out of the corner of his eye he spied the Chrysler Building, Rockefeller Plaza, the Empire State, the famous library, the lights of Times Square, and other famous monuments. How he longed to fly in closer and look them over.

But he wasn't there as a tourist.

That must be it, he thought, as a building loomed in front of him. It was good thing he'd been told to follow the park. There were so many high-rises, so many lights, so many trains and cars and buses, so many billboards and other distractions that it would have been easy to lose his bearings.

Below him was a structure that sprawled for half a city block. It was twenty storeys tall and had lots of vents and fans on its roof, way too many for a residential complex. The back of the building didn't tell him much, so he steered the pigeon lower, to the front entrance on the east side of 10th. There was a sign sure enough: ST. LUKE'S ROOSEVELT.

He drew close to an ornate entrance and scanned its heights, which consisted of light-coloured brick and a grid of windows. Were some of them open? There. On the fourteenth floor one was open a crack. Parking the pigeon on a nearby ledge, Simon quit its vadh and entered the hospital in kaba form. He found himself in a small room with two narrow beds. Each held a sleeping senior with tubes and wires running from their limbs. Stealing past them, Simon shot into a hallway that was cluttered with a line of trays on wheels, monitors, walkers, and a linen cart. There was also an old lady seated in a wheelchair and a man in a suit standing beside her.

"I'll get you some water, Mom, and then I'll go. They don't like visitors staying later than they should."

The lady said nothing. She was old and wrinkled, and her body was wasted. To judge by her expressionless eyes, she had Alzheimer's or some similar condition. Her weakness worked to Simon's advantage. As her son stepped away from the chair, Simon closed in on her shatl.

"Who are you?" her kaba swiftly demanded.

Before he could answer, it asked, *"Who am I?"*

"I'm Simon," he answered. *"Would you like a ride?"*

"A ride? That would be lovely. But who's going to push? That young man has gone and left me alone."

"He's off to get some water. You and I will push together."

Without further ado, he set her hands on the wheelchair's rims. Concentrating hard, he managed to get them working. At first their progress was slow, but soon they were moving at a pretty good clip. Twice they almost crashed into something, but Simon was able to steer them clear. After travelling fifty metres, they drew up to an elevator. Hanging on one wall was a map of the building, much to Simon's satisfaction.

He looked it over quickly. The maternity ward was two floors down. He pressed a button and waited for the lift to appear.

"Where's that man?" the lady asked. *"He's very nice."*

"He is very nice," Simon agreed. *"He called you 'Mom' so he must be your son."*

"I don't remember," the kaba moaned. *"But I'm sure I love him. Isn't that odd?"*

The elevator came and he wheeled them aboard. Two nurses were chatting and Simon asked them for floor twelve. He spoke to them in the woman's voice, which was gravelly and surprisingly low.

When the doors for the twelfth floor opened, he wheeled them down an immaculate hallway. Following signs to the birthing centre, he drew them up to his destination.

"Babies!" the kaba cried. *"I love babies. Especially newborns."*

"They're very sweet," Simon agreed.

They were poised before a long picture window. Behind the glass were thirty bassinets on wheels. Each bassinet contained a single baby. Some were large, some tiny, some bald, some full of hair. Half were in pink blankets, the others in blue.

A heavy nurse was exiting the room. Before the door could close completely, Simon left the lady and wandered inside.

The babies seemed okay, Simon thought. A few were flailing their arms about and groaning, twisting and making faces, but for the most part they seemed peaceful. They were adorable too and he had to smile.

Although …

He studied them more carefully. Something was off. While five were squirming and grunting and burping, the rest were lying very still. Not only that, but the five "troublemakers" had their eyes half closed while the remainder were staring wide-eyed at the ceiling. They all bore smiles.

He drew up to a baby girl and looked into her pupils. He jumped back in shock. No doubt about it. There was something alien behind her eyes, something intelligent, ancient, and far from friendly. As if sensing Simon's kaba, the newborn bared its gums.

The bolkhs had won themselves twenty-five limnls.

Simon wanted out of there. Luckily enough, the nurse had returned and, as the door opened briefly, Simon escaped. He plunged into the lady again and shoved off from the window, as if fleeing the carnage of an accident scene. Those poor, poor newborns. They'd been murdered as soon as they'd drawn their first breath.

Steering the wheelchair down the hall, he spied a women's washroom and approached it quickly. If Jenny were scattering clues behind, chances were she would have left one there, immediately beside the scene of the crime. Propping the chair against the door, Simon inspected the space.

Sure enough, he found a gob of spit and a message from Jenny, "Sloane Hosp mat ward."

He returned to the lady and got the wheelchair rolling. He felt like puking. There were more wards to visit before he caught up with Tarhlo, and that meant examining more murder scenes. He wondered if his nerves could take it.

They were poised by the elevators. As Simon debated his next course of action a door popped open and the woman's son emerged. With him was a pair of nurses. The son's look of worry turned to one of relief as soon as he spied his aged mother. The nurses couldn't help but laugh, amused that she had managed to elude them.

"How did you do it?" the man asked, embracing his mother. "I didn't think you could wander the hallways."

"She's a deep one," one of the nurses said. "You might not think it, but she's still busy in that head of hers."

"I just wish she could hear me," the son said sadly. "I'll bet she thinks she's a burden on me. But I love these visits. I wish I could tell her."

"You don't have to," Simon spoke, on behalf of the lady. "I know you love seeing me and I'm blessed to have a son like you. Even when my memory's gone, my love for you will be here always. Remember that for the two of us."

The son's jaw dropped and the nurses were gasping. With this message delivered, Simon left the lady's shatl.

He had a long night's work ahead of him still.

The sun was dissolving the shadows. Pigeons were already beginning to stir. Three of them were wandering near Simon's feet, hoping he had some crumbs to feed them. The traffic was mounting and people were strolling, morning cups of coffee in hand. Most were headed for City Hall, located to the left of Simon. The light was striking its limestone front, and its stairs and portico looked grand and inviting. The hubbub was rising as the city prepared itself for another day. An electric current hung in the air: there was money to be made, or so a Wall Street suit suggested as he walked by Simon with a look of disapproval.

Simon was on a bench in City Hall Park, close to the junction of Park Row and Broadway, poised in the shadow of the Woolworth Building. His mood was hardly cheerful.

He was bone, bone tired. After leaving St. Luke's, he'd travelled to the Sloane Maternity Hospital, a few blocks away from the George Washington Bridge. There he'd encountered close to forty newborns whose kabas had been ousted and replaced by bolkhs. Another clue from Jenny had directed him to the Lenox Hill maternity ward, where the bolkhs had struck again. From there he'd proceeded to Bellevue Hospital, where another forty-two newborns had been hijacked. That brought the total to a hundred and thirty, and Tarhlo had been operating for just one day.

Jenny's final clue had read, "Downtown Hosp, morning." Simon inferred from this note that they'd quit for the evening, gone to a hotel, and would resume once visiting hours started the next day. He was seated there in City Hall Park because their next target was two blocks off. In an hour or so there would be a showdown.

Simon bit his nails. His shatl was a thirty-year-old man whom he'd nabbed at Bellevue two hours before. He'd had several candidates to choose from in the emergency ward. There'd been five drunks, three heroin addicts, two gunshot victims, a schizophrenic, an older woman who was mumbling nonsense, and a man who'd died of a heart attack in the middle of jogging. Examining these shatls, Simon had gone for the dead man: not only could he control him for as long as he needed, but the guy was carrying a wad of cash. He hated using the dead like this but was doing so for the sake of the living.

The last few days were starting to tell on Simon. While he needed all his strength to deal with Tarhlo, the news of his origins, his travels across Europe, his uncle's capture, the kabas in Clara, the attacks on the newborns, and the coming showdown, all were weighing him down. But what really ate at him was the Carpenters. If he could explain himself to his former family, how he'd never intended to deceive anyone and was grateful for the years he'd spent with them, everything would seem a little less hopeless. Even if the odds were stacked against him. But why would the Carpenters waste their kindness on him? Because of him they'd been deprived of their son and forced to rear some ghostly caveman.

And yet … He looked at his hands, the ones belonging to the jogger. Maybe the guy had been a horrible jerk. Maybe he'd been a lousy dad, son, and husband. But if a doctor phoned his loved ones up and told them he'd made a terrible mistake, that their dad, son, and husband was alive and kicking? Wouldn't they greet the news with joy? So maybe the Carpenters would be glad if he gave them a call. And even if they were upset, it would do him good to hear their voices.

He climbed to his feet. A minute later he was standing in a phone booth and asking the operator to place a collect call. After punching in his mom's cell number, he waited breathlessly as a phone started ringing.

"Hello?" his mother, Ms. Carpenter, spoke.

"There's a collect call from Simon," the operator said. "Do you accept the charges?"

"Yes! Of course!" Ms. Carpenter cried. "Simon? Are you okay?"

"Yes. Listen, Mom, I mean, Phyllis ..."

"Don't you dare!" she yelled indignantly. "How dare you call me anything but Mom! I raised you from birth! I held you, fed you, and put you to sleep. Can you guess how many happy times we've shared? Don't you dare think of taking those riches away!"

"But you must know ..."

"I have a new son. His name is Si, to distinguish him from you. But we didn't gain one son only to lose another!"

"I ... I ... But what if I visit in a stranger's body? What if ..."

"We don't care! Do you hear? We don't care! We'll welcome you in any shape, size, or colour! Just come back as soon as you can, day or night, spring or fall! Do you hear, my love? Do you understand?"

Simon swallowed hard. When he finally spoke, he asked if the others were okay. His mother told him they were back at home. Emma had left a letter with Si, explaining how their babies' kabas had been swapped.

She'd apologized profusely and assured them that the danger had passed. Tarhlo wasn't interested in them. So everything was normal now, except that he was absent and they missed him terribly. Luckily his body was with them still, even if someone new was inside.

"And you?" she asked. "Are you okay?"

"I am now," he answered, with a bark of laughter. "I could fight an army on my own if I had to."

Chapter Twenty

Simon took a deep breath. Still buried in the heart attack victim, he stepped inside a revolving door, a new knapsack in hand. The talk with his mother had done him good. Not only were his nerves less strained, but his blood was up and he was feeling optimistic. Because his head was clear he'd come up with a plan — not a great one, necessarily, but a plan nonetheless. To make it work he need "equipment." After talking with his mother, Simon had done some shopping, taking advantage of the cash in the jogger's pockets.

In the hospital foyer a guard scanned him briefly. He didn't like what he saw and waved him over.

"Can I help you?"

"I would like to go upstairs. My wife just had a baby."

"Visiting hours don't start until ten."

"I'd really like to see her."

"You and everyone else," the guard said snidely. "A group just asked to go up early. What do folks think this is? Grand Central Station?"

"When was this?"

"I don't know. Twenty minutes ago."

"Does that mean I can go up too?"

"Yeah, okay. Fifth floor, on your right. And, sir?"

"Yes?" Simon asked with a note of worry.

"Congratulations."

Simon smiled weakly and approached the elevators. Some patients and staff were milling about but they didn't pay him any notice, unaware that they were rubbing shoulders with a dead man. The elevator opened and there was a gurney inside. On it was an older man who was knocked out cold.

As they climbed to the fifth floor, Simon glanced at the gurney. Because the guy was unconscious he could have been hijacked; no, with so many bolkhs at large he *should* have been hijacked. But as far as he could tell, the bolkhs hadn't touched him.

"Why nab him," Simon thought, "when they can be limnls?"

They arrived at the fifth floor and the metal door opened. Simon exited and was alone in the hallway. From his bag he took a pair of headphones, ones that would cancel out any background noises (that's at least what the packaging said). When he'd put them on he pulled out something else.

Simon had found a cassette player in a shop on Broadway. Amazed that these were still available, he pressed his luck further and asked if the store sold tapes as well. A tired-looking clerk had led him to a bin full of tapes featuring all kinds of music. Because Simon hated music he had no idea what he was looking for. That's why he had asked the clerk, "Can you recommend something that would grate on someone's nerves?" The clerk had stared at him as if he were nuts. With a shrug, he'd quickly chosen *The Bob Dylan Collection.* "This is something you either hate or love," he'd said, "and if you hate it, it will drive you bonkers."

Simon placed the tape into the player, the way a hunter loads shells into a shotgun's chambers. Making sure the player's batteries were in, he took it in hand and continued forward. His "weapon" gave him confidence.

A door marked off the maternity ward. Pausing outside, he reached into his bag again and removed a bottle containing a milk-white fluid. He inhaled deeply and wished himself luck. Opening the door he crossed its threshold.

He'd been bracing for the sight of Tarhlo, but it was still shocking when Simon spied him in the flesh, together with his travel companions.

Simon counted twelve of them. Jenny and Emma were seated in an alcove, along with eight women who were definitely hemindhs. They were nicely dressed and properly groomed, but their expressions and posture showed that something was off, that there was madness beneath their mascara and lipstick. Four of the faces were deathly pale, as if these crones had been invalids before they were snatched.

Tarhlo was three paces away with his back to Simon. It was easy to see that his shatl was different. The one before had been dark and slender, while this one was ruddy and had a boxer's build. The switch made sense. His old shatl couldn't travel without papers and obtaining them would have been far from easy. He'd travelled inside Clara and found a shatl on landing.

And Clara? She was standing a few feet to the right of Tarhlo. Her limbs and features were unnaturally still — from the smakho, Simon thought. Her eyes were directed on a window before her, behind which lay more bassinets on wheels. There were nineteen of them altogether, each with a newborn in a blue or pink blanket. The scene was peaceful, but Simon almost retched.

The babies were being ousted even as he watched. A door to the ward lay on the far side of Clara and a wooden chair was propping it open. The bolkhs were invisible to the naked eye, but for sure they were swooping into the ward. And while they couldn't be seen, their actions could. The newborns were twitching, not in the way that babies do, but with a wildness that suggested they were fighting to survive. They were. The bolkhs were tearing into them and kicking out their kabas — like snails or turtles being ripped from their shells. These frail luras were putting up a fight but the bolkhs were pitiless and the newborns were — newborns.

It was easy to see when a bolkh won out. After shaking violently and tossing his limbs, the baby would grow eerily still and lie on his back with his eyes wide open.

The sight was so disgusting that Simon gasped. In the silence it sounded like a gun going off and attracted everyone's eyes to him — Emma's, Jenny's, the hemindhs' … and Tarhlo's.

Their gazes met. Tarhlo knew Simon instantly. He was riding in the jogger but his father wasn't fooled. His reaction was faster than the eye could follow. Leaping at Simon he punched him hard. The blow caught Simon square on the jaw and pitched him into the door behind him. Before he could recover, Tarhlo struck twice more, thrusting himself between Simon and Clara. Sensing danger, the hemindhs were moving in closer, while Jenny and Emma were standing too.

Everything seemed to unfold in slow motion, as though air in the room had suddenly turned to caramel. Tarhlo's shatl was tensing his muscles, a sign that he was preparing to strike again. The hemindhs were rushing in a mass at Simon, except for three whom Emma and Jenny were fighting; Jenny was battling two at once. As Tarhlo's fist came flying toward Simon, two hemindhs leapt in his direction. Everyone was screaming in comic silence (Simon's headphones prevented any sound from leaking in). Simon took action. His finger pressed a button and the tape deck started playing.

Simon was glad his headphones were the soundproof type. Judging by Tarhlo's pained expression, the music was poison. The sounds bombarded him from everywhere at once, and he dropped to his knees and started screaming in anguish. His hands were on his ears but the noise leaked through. While the hemindhs were only slightly affected, they were shocked to see their leader so helpless. They turned away from Simon and tried to help Tarhlo.

A nurse entered the room just then. Simon saw her ask, "What's going on?" Aware that she was badly outnumbered she turned and ran into the depths of the ward, to phone the security desk downstairs, most likely.

While the bolkhs were distracted, Simon stepped toward Clara. Holding the recorder between his knees, he unscrewed the cap off the bottle and motioned her to drink. She was too far gone on smakho to react. Squeezing her nostrils, he brought the bottle to her lips. When her mouth fell open, he poured the contents in.

Some spilled to the floor but most got in. The blend of milk, oregano, and thyme neutralized the smakho and brought her up sharply. She blinked and stretched, like Snow White awakening from the witch's spell. She was alert enough to drink on her own, so he handed her the bottle and waited by her side.

That's when five of the hemindhs struck. Enraged that he was interfering, they lunged at him. Simon wasn't much of a fighter. All he could do was steel his shatl to withstand their blows. But that's when something happened. The hemindhs seemed to miss their target. It was as if an unseen hand had grabbed them and thrown them against the window — the reinforced glass just managed to hold. Two jumped back up and got between Simon and Clara. From there they were able to strike at Simon.

One scratched him in the face while the other punched his sternum. As Simon doubled over, his fist swung out and struck a hemindh's skull, breaking at least a couple of the jogger's fingers. Undaunted, Simon kicked three times. He was able to bring one hag down, but he missed the second time and lost his balance on the third. The two hemindhs jumped him, clawing with their nails. He elbowed one, but two more piled on. Jenny and Emma weren't able to help — Emma had her hands full and Jenny was half-pinned to the floor. The hags were getting the better of them.

But …

Simon happened to roll near Clara and the hemindhs attacking him were tossed aside, as if a hand had come to Simon's rescue. They regained their feet and ran at him again, only to fly off at a sixty-degree angle, all without him having to lift a finger. Three times this happened. Why?

He thought of that picture that he'd seen in Paris, showing the woplh and hamax with a circle around them. He suddenly understood its meaning. This was his power. If he stood near Clara, he could generate this field and keep everyone at bay. He could save them both from any assailant, like an umbrella repelling a heavy rain. What had Cletho said, back in the cave? That it wouldn't be smart to mix the woplh and hamax? That's why Tarhlo had kept them apart, in the domh and while hiking to that car on Gibraltar. Together they were strong. No — together they were invincible.

This realization distracted him. A hemindh just managed to drag him back from Clara. Worse, she was able to grab his headphones. They fell to the floor and a wall of sound struck home. Simon imagined it was lot like being hit by a bus. People were shouting, grunting, cursing. Chairs were flying. Tarhlo was howling. But the music hurt the most by far.

The noises didn't sound human at all. The guitar was like acid burning into his kaba. The singer's voice sliced through Simon and mashed all his organs together. The harmonica was turning his bones to mush and setting all his nerves on fire. Simon felt dizzy, empty, drained of hope. His will couldn't keep his shatl erect and he reeled and tottered to the tiled floor, like a jet being forced to make a crash landing.

And then the music stopped.

Simon looked up groggily. One hag had seized the player and switched it off. She removed the cassette and tore it with her nails, ensuring that it couldn't be played again. Simon was trying to clear his kaba, while his shatl was attempting to get off the floor. A foot kicked his ribs and knocked him over. As he tried to rise a second time, the same foot laid him low.

Tarhlo.

Simon's "dad" was standing over him, eyeing him closely. Tarhlo's expression was cold, murderous even. Three hemindhs had Emma and Jenny beaten: their arms were pinned behind their backs. The other hemindhs were holding hands and forming a closed ring around Simon. He immediately thought of the exhibit in Paris and the picture that Michel had shown him and Earl. What was his theory about this ring? That it would prevent a kaba from escaping a vessel? He reached out with his senses. Yes. He could feel the hemindhs' will about him, solid as a concrete wall. No one moved and no one spoke. After the fury of the last two minutes, this lull was almost laughable.

Tarhlo waved a hemindh closer. She passed him a flask, which he deftly opened. Simon could smell the smakho within. What now? Oh. His father was going to make him drink, so that they could knock him out and leave him stranded. The group would travel somewhere else, making sure they couldn't be followed this time.

Tarhlo yanked Simon up and pressed the flask to his mouth. He was smiling vindictively as he made to pour the smakho down. A drop of it and Simon would be out for the count. Tarhlo's mouth was open to jeer at Simon, but exactly then a hand touched his shoulder. It was thin and white, the hand of a girl, but suggestive of enormous power.

Clara. She'd been drinking Simon's brew all along and flushed every trace of smakho from her system. Tarhlo was gripping him tightly still, but Simon managed to catch her expression: it was a mix of sadness, regret, confusion, but above all else there was a burning anger.

"Krahla," Tarhlo spoke, taken aback, "this doesn't concern you."

Clara stared fiercely and struggled to speak. Simon didn't think she was up to the task.

"Krahla," Tarhlo went on, in a cajoling way, "don't interfere. I won't harm Krahl. I'm just putting him to sleep."

She refused to back away. Her lips kept moving.

"Krahla," he said impatiently, "we're wasting time. Please step back."

"Leave," she finally managed to say.

"Leave? Of course," Tarhlo said with a laugh. "We've sown as many limnls as we can and it's time we headed to our next destination."

"Leave," she repeated, with greater force.

"Yes. Good idea. Let's get going. We'll give Krahl this drink and …"

"Leave," she screamed. "Leave! Leave! Leave!"

That's when he realized she wasn't talking to him.

Chapter Twenty-One

Kabas can't be seen or heard. But what's true of one kaba, or even a dozen, isn't true of thousands of them — not inside a tiny room at least. Or so Simon learned over the next few seconds.

Now that she was free of smakho, Clara controlled her "gates" again. She could admit any kaba, or expel them at will. This applied to the bolkhs inside her. The very moment she told them to leave, it was as if a bouncer were kicking them into the cold.

Simon raised his hands protectively, there was such a flurry of shapes about him. A stream of shadows abandoned Clara and cluttered the room, unseen, unheard, but unquestionably there. Simon could feel them pulsing around him, flitting against the walls and ceiling, bashing into chairs and tables in their anxiety to find new vadhs. There was an aura of fear, rage, and desperation — desperation most of all — as they circled about aimlessly, their one shelter gone and no substitute in sight. As unbearably close as their presence was, more kept streaming from Clara's hollows.

Tarhlo was looking on in distress, like a man whose house is covered in flames. The hemindhs were wailing and beating their heads, as if a massacre were occurring before their very eyes. Still more kabas retreated from Clara, their frenzy growing with each passing second.

Despite his shock, Tarhlo reacted calmly: he opened a door to let the kabas escape and find themselves new vessels to hide in. Sure enough, they rushed outside and filled the fifth-floor hallways. Not that this would save them. If more doors weren't opened, they would fly about in vain and quickly weaken. Tarhlo was trapped. He could stay with the hamax or he could let his people die. The second choice was out of the question. That's why he cursed and ran from the room, followed by a couple of hemindhs. Moments later there was the sound of windows being smashed.

Simon knew he had to act. Tarhlo would come rushing back shortly, and the kabas would find themselves vadhs and shatls. Within minutes hordes would start to gather, intent on drugging Clara again.

Before the remaining hags could stop him, Simon grabbed Clara's hand. He felt a crackle ripple around them and inside his shatl his kaba glowed. Alarmed that Simon was touching the hamax, the hemindhs attacked. An instant later all went flying and crashed into the walls.

"Are you okay?" Simon asked his mother.

"I'm fine," Emma answered. "How did you find us?"

"I had help from Jenny," he said, throwing his cousin a smile.

Jenny answered with a feeble grin. She'd taken a few knocks. Her forehead was bleeding and her ankle was twisted to the point she couldn't walk on it. As she limped to Simon and hugged him briefly, he wondered how she'd be able to keep up. They couldn't leave her, but they had to move quickly.

His worries were groundless.

Touching him, Jenny felt her strength return. Her forehead stopped bleeding and her ankle straightened. Simon couldn't believe it, until he realized his broken hand wasn't troubling him either.

He recalled Michel's words, how he and Clara would bring out strengths in each other. This capacity to heal was one of them, he figured. But this wasn't the time to take stock of their powers.

"Let's move," he said.

"Where to?" Emma asked.

"We'll figure that out later. Let's escape this building before the bolkhs regroup."

They passed into the hallway. Tarhlo was visible but his hands were full. Guards had arrived in answer to the nurse's call, and Tarhlo and the hemindhs were fighting them off. The battle was desperate. Glad for this distraction, Simon fled the scene. Leading the group past several doors, he came upon a concrete stairwell. Jenny started falling behind. As soon as she was out of their orbit, her forehead started bleeding and her ankle acted up again.

"Don't lag!" Simon warned. "Keep holding hands, no matter what!"

As they descended the stairs, they heard footsteps above. More hemindhs were approaching. The hospital was full of lakhn patients and the wandering bolkhs had taken them over. If the group didn't leave, they would soon be surrounded.

They emerged on the ground floor and were greeted with chaos. When Tarhlo had smashed the windows upstairs, the bolkhs had escaped and flitted down to street level where they'd hijacked the closest available vessels. Animals were storming the building — dogs, cats, squirrels, rats, anything the bolkhs had been able to find. There were homeless folk too, of every size and description. The foyer was packed and still the hemindhs kept coming. The guards tried to hold them back but were brutally set on and neutralized. Two were unconscious and the bolkhs nabbed them too.

A toothless hag spotted them first. She screamed and the mob zeroed in on Simon. The elevators were blocked, the exits were blocked, the central hallway was blocked ... but not the passage to emergency. Dodging between a series of gurneys, Simon led them down a gleaming hallway, pausing only to close a door and wedge an empty wheelchair against it. Moments later they were in the emergency ward. At its far end was a bay where an ambulance stood idling.

From a side door a pack of dogs came rushing in. Spying the group they hurtled forward, growling and barking and baring their fangs. A greyhound leapt at them, a Doberman, a Lab, and a tiny chihuahua. They flew through the air, their teeth clacking in anger. Simon focused and pitched them backward, smashing them into chairs, walls, and medical equipment. The clatter was ear-splitting.

They reached a bay and sidled past its door. A man attached to an IV followed and took a vicious swing at them. Beside him was a boy with his arms in a cast. Both were tossed like rag dolls. On the far side of the room more hemindhs appeared and the dogs were preparing to rush them again.

They had to leave. Quickly. Glancing round feverishly, Simon spied the ambulance. Its engine was idling, as if inviting them to enter. Could he?

Yes.

"Get inside!" he yelled. "But keep holding hands! Enter through the driver's door!"

The women went ahead of him. As they installed themselves, he fought a second wave of dogs, as well as squirrels jumping down from the rafters and birds dive-bombing him from every side at once. And a mass of humans was approaching.

"Get in!" Emma yelled.

Simon swung into the driver's seat and closed the door. Just in time. Hemindhs collided with the vehicle's sides and hammered its windows recklessly. They smashed hands and fingers in their frenzy to break in. The glass started buckling.

"Let's go!" Emma cried.

Setting the vehicle in gear, Simon stepped on the gas. The tires screeched and they pitched forward, knocking down a hemindh who was about to dash a chair into the windscreen.

He pulled into Beekman Street, narrowly avoiding a cab. As it screeched to a stop and the driver started honking, Simon saw four hemindhs charge it. They opened a door, dragged the driver outside and, an instant later, the cab was racing toward them. At the same time birds knocked into the windshield in an attempt to throw the ambulance off balance. Dogs were tearing furiously behind.

He reached Beekman and Nassau. Frantic to leave these bolkhs behind, he hung a right then a left, ending up on Spruce Street. Roaring past a stop sign, he grazed a Honda Civic, provoking another volley of honking. The Honda was about to give chase but the cab rammed into it, sending it flying.

"There are bolkhs in that cab," Emma warned. "And watch those dogs!"

Every dog they passed would abandon its owner and take off after them. The same was true of mad-men, drunks, and any kaba that was lakhn. A shirtless man tossed a bottle their way. A ragged woman shoved a buggy in their path. Simon had to swerve and hit a bin full of books. As a stream of paper filled the air, he turned left onto Park Row.

A line of cars confronted them. The cab was half a block behind, and so was a truck with a hemindh at its wheel that was smashing anything in its path.

Simon jumped the pavement to avoid the traffic. A hotdog vendor leapt aside and screamed as the ambulance wrecked his stand. A drunk assailed them with a stroller, and a pack of dogs tried to bite the tires.

Simon regained the road and veered onto Barclay. A cyclist and a dozen cars were hemming him in. He wove between them with amazing precision, as if they were moving in slow motion. With Clara next to him, he knew just what to do. The dumptruck and cab weren't nearly as graceful: the cab wound up striking a pole, while the dumptruck crashed into the steps of a church.

"That's amazing," Emma gasped. "The Carpenters should see you driving now!"

Simon smiled grimly.

He entered Church Street. The cab and truck had fallen behind, but they still weren't in the clear. A flock of birds was on their trail and hemindhs were appearing on the sidewalk in droves. They passed a woman walking six dogs. All six broke free and set off in pursuit. And as they approached the next intersection, the hemindhs formed three lines. Each blocked a street off, forcing them to turn on Warren.

"What are they doing?" Emma cried.

"They're coralling us," Simon yelled, making the turn. "They don't care if we hit them. They'll survive even if their shatls don't. But they're assuming I won't kill these people, not if I can help it. So the vadhs and shatls can steer us where they want."

Warren ended at City Hall Park. They could only turn right or left on Broadway, or so the raging hemindhs thought. They numbered in the dozens, had their hands linked together, and were all grinning widely, certain that Simon had no place to go. If he turned he would crush a lot of innocent shatls — including kids and a very young baby. He was trapped and clearly theirs for the plucking.

"We're stuck unless we run them over," Emma cried.

"I can't do that."

"Of course you can't," she agreed.

"So we're sunk," Jenny said.

"No," Simon said. "There's always the park!"

The light at the end of Warren was green. Picking up speed, Simon drove across Broadway. Honking furiously, he aimed for the sidewalk ahead. Normal people were hanging about, wondering what this commotion meant and why a large crowd was blocking traffic on Broadway. When they saw an ambulance flying toward them, they jumped to one side, just managing to dodge it. That's when Simon jumped the curb and wound up on a walkway leading into the park, grazing its wrought-iron gate in the process.

People were visiting City Hall or the courts. He saw panicked faces pass in a blur. Well-dressed luras scrambled into bushes and a woman spilled her coffee as she mounted a wall. Everyone was desperate to avoid being struck, not only by the ambulance but by the wave of hemindhs running behind it. They were like a herd of cattle stampeding.

They were almost across the park. Centre Street was fast approaching and Simon was wondering what his next step was. A sign zipped by. It pointed to the Brooklyn Bridge.

The bus appeared from out of thin air. As they reached a square at the end of the park, the bus rammed them at an oblique angle. The ambulance spun, skidded wildly, and wound up bashing into a wooden fruit stand. The collision wasn't terrible but the ambulance was finished.

The driver alighted. He was bearded and dressed in a getup so ragged that it was amazing it didn't fall to the ground. He walked toward the ambulance, taking long, graceful steps. Despite his appearance, he moved like a king.

Tarhlo.

"Outside!" Simon yelled, clambering to the sidewalk. "And keep holding hands!"

"Where now?" Emma asked, standing beside him.

"Just follow me!"

Crossing Centre Street, they entered the bridge's promenade. Three hemindhs tried to block them but he scattered them like bowling pins.

They were sprinting. Clara couldn't keep up so Simon took her on his back, not once slackening his hold on Emma. He was surprised how light his sister felt; she was weightless, in fact. When she wrapped her arms about him, his kaba glowed with such raw energy that he was sure the jogger's body was about to catch flame.

He felt weirdly calm. The luras on the bridge were eyeing them suspiciously, as if grasping there was something odd about the group. Sirens tore the air, a sign the cops were closing in. Tarhlo was on their tail with a legion of bolkhs. Simon hadn't a clue where he was headed or how he would escape this situation — in other words, things were desperate. And yet, deep inside, he was calm, even happy. When he glanced back at Manhattan, he was only thinking how beautiful the city looked. How odd. They were in a terrible jam yet he'd never felt so tranquil.

This was Clara's doing. With his twin on his back, he was finally complete. Nature had fashioned them to complement each other and now, at long last, they were fitted together. He could have flitted off and never been found. He could have abandoned his shatl, left New York City, wandered to the far side of the globe, and done well for himself. But he wouldn't. He couldn't. His place was there, beside his sister. He would sooner die a million times than be parted from his sibling.

Except.

The bridge's first tower was fast approaching and there were frenzied shouts ahead. Around the tower a crowd was gathered — a familiar one of vadhs and shatls. They numbered in the hundreds and more were arriving. They were laying siege to the path before them.

"It's no better behind," Emma said.

Simon wheeled indifferently. Sure enough, a sea of hemindhs was dogging them closely, with Tarhlo in front. He was too far off to see his face clearly, but Simon guessed his father was grinning.

A helicopter hovered above. There were cruisers at both ends of the bridge and police boats guarded the river below. The bolkhs paid the cops no notice. They couldn't care less what any lura thought.

Below them were four lanes of heavy traffic. *How funny*, Simon thought. The drivers weren't aware of the commotion above.

Dogs rushed forward from the bridge's Brooklyn side. When they were ten feet off, they struck Simon's "wall" and went flying back into the hemindhs' ranks. Tightening his grip on Emma, Simon pressed on. As he advanced, the bolkhs were forced to give ground.

At first the task was manageable. The hemindhs were loosely packed and easy to dislodge. But bit by bit their masses thickened and more and more shatls rushed up from behind. Their weight was growing and Simon was having to strain. He'd gained the first tower but his shatl was shaking. He muscled on, like a bulldozer pushing against an increasing mound of earth — eventually its mass would bring the engine to a stop.

Ten more metres gained. The cop in the chopper was yelling something. Some birds assailed Simon from above, bouncing against his field, breaking their wings and dropping to the bridge in droves. Clara's mouth was near his ear. She was breathing softly and smelled vaguely of thyme.

Another ten metres. Simon was feeling light-headed but happy still. Whether they escaped or not, his task was simple. To strain until he could go no further.

"Watch it!" his mother yelled. "They're attacking from behind!"

From behind, Simon thought in a daze. Okay. He'd

deal with them too. His kaba laboured and the sky grew brighter. From far off he heard his mother shouting, while Clara's breathing was soft and even.

"Stop! Let me address my children!"

Tarhlo's voice rang out like a trumpet. He was speaking through the ragged man, but there was no mistaking his forceful presence. As the bolkhs drew back at their leader's command, Simon stopped straining and looked around. Jenny and Emma instinctively drew nearer, while Clara dropped to the ground to give him a rest. They were trapped between two armies and there were luras to deal with. Simon got his bearings: Brooklyn was on his left, Manhattan on his right. Beneath them the flow of traffic was constant. Their motion was causing the bridge to vibrate.

"My children," Tarhlo boomed, from a short way off, "first, you must know how proud I am. You're fighting your own kin, but your exploits do the Khalkons proud."

He paused. The chopper was trying to swoop in closer. At a nod from Tarhlo birds swarmed the machine. The pilot got the message and retreated instantly.

"But this battle has ended, as you must know. We are many and you are four. Even if the woplh is strong, how long can he withstand our fury? If he thrusts five thousand vadhs from the hamax, we will find five thousand more. And if you escape this bridge? Where will you hide? Where can you go where we won't find you? We have the might of the wind, the sun's raw power, the patience of the earth, and the rain's soft cunning. Stalemate is the very best you can hope for."

Tarhlo paused to let his words sink in. The city's background sounds intruded: honking, yelling, countless people going about their business, unaware that their future was being decided. A future that was looking more and more bleak. Jenny and Emma were starting to wilt. Clara was blank. Simon felt serene.

"But why should *we* be satisfied with stalemate?" Tarhlo resumed. "Why should we give in to your resistance? We can't defeat you here, but we can, and will destroy these vadhs and shatls. We can throw them into the river or stand in the path of oncoming cars or jump from buildings onto crowds of luras. The means of inflicting death are many. And despite my reluctance to prove so cruel, that will be our course of action, right here, right now, if the hamax doesn't return to us. You wish to keep the luras safe? We will kill them ruthlessly if you don't join us. You will let us use our hamax as nature intended. Otherwise ..."

Simon's calmness left him and nausea took over. So running from Tarhlo had been useless from the start. His father was right. Nature had built them to incarnate bolkhs, even if this meant the luras would suffer. If they struggled, luras would die. If they surrendered, luras would fade over time. There was no third way ...

Or was there?

While Tarhlo had been talking, Clara had wandered over to the railing. It was designed to keep pedestrians from tumbling to the traffic below. No one noticed how she'd gripped the railing, how she'd lifted her body, how she looked with longing at the marvels of Manhattan and the sun's transcendent glory as it reached its zenith. No one noticed … and when they did it was too late.

"Clara!" Emma shrieked, as the hamax jumped.

Clara was special. There had not been a hamax in over ten thousand years. She was rarer than the finest wines, the purest gold, the choicest jewels. Yet her body still fell like a stone.

Simon was after her in a heartbeat, sped on by five thousand cries of anguish. A woplh is just as rare as a hamax, yet he too fell like any common pebble.

As he flew through the air in the wake of his sister, he was aware of the silence that was preparing to clasp them. It lay between the blasts of horns and shuddering metal and shrieking brakes, between luras and bolkhs screaming in horror, between the wail of sirens, the chopper's blades turning, and the river lapping against the bridge's stone blocks. They were falling, falling. It took an eternity to travel to the lane below and, as much as Simon tried to hurry, he couldn't catch up to his twin sister. The engulfing silence kept them apart.

He saw her hit the roadway hard. He saw her legs buckle and her torso shake and her skull strike a surface that was cruel and unforgiving. And that was the easiest part by far. She was in the path of a pickup truck that was speeding forward at fifty miles per hour. It would crush her every bone and organ and leave nothing of her rareness behind.

Except that Simon drew his shatl about her. Except that his kaba managed to link with hers. Except that he generated just enough force to sustain the pent-up shock of the truck and, in the blink of an eye, bring it to a standstill. Over a dozen cars collided. The city's skyline shuddered and the noonday sky was filled with curses. But he'd been true to his word and guarded his sister.

"I didn't fail you," he whispered, as a mass of blackness closed in.

Chapter Twenty-Two

It was drizzling lightly. Simon loved to watch the rain on the window. A nurse had left it open a crack and the sound of the traffic passing outside was like waves crashing against a shore, reminding Simon of his life in Vancouver and a set of routines that was his no longer. Not that he minded. He had Clara now.

She wasn't well. Both her legs had broken in the fall and she would be in traction for weeks, maybe months. Her spleen was ruptured and one kidney might fail. She was bruised all over and her skull was fractured.

These injuries weren't the chief concern. Most worrying was the fact that she was in a coma. Day and night her eyes gaped open, unblinking, expressionless, and unresponsive. The nurses changed her bandages. Nothing. The doctors poked her and shined lights in her eyes. Nothing. Jenny and Emma sat by her side, addressing her softly and stroking her limbs. Nothing. And when Simon leapt inside her, he could never see her kaba. Back and forth he'd wander her hollows, but he never caught a glimpse of it. It was like visiting a mansion that the owner has abandoned.

That's not to say her hollows were empty. Over a hundred kabas were contained within. At first their presence puzzled Simon, until he realized they were the newborns whom the bolkhs had ousted. Refusing to take part in their murder, Clara had generously hauled them in.

A radio was playing somewhere in the background. The station was a local one and a panel was debating the events from three weeks back. They'd been so strange and crazy that New Yorkers were discussing them still. Why had homeless people gathered on the bridge? Why had that young girl jumped? What was her link to the mysterious jogger who'd saved her life at the cost of his own? Why did he match the description of a man who'd died the night before over in Bellevue? And how had the pickup truck stopped so quickly? People were concocting the wildest theories and conspiracy freaks would be busy for years.

There was a sound at the door and Emma and Jenny stepped in. Visiting hours had just begun. They always appeared at the start of the day and would stay until the last possible moment. Earl would arrive at some point or another. As soon as he'd learned what had happened to Clara, he'd caught the first plane from Paris. No bolkh had bothered stopping him. While he spent as much time as he could with the girls, someone had to look after the bills. He'd travel to Atlantic City each day and visit the casinos.

"Good morning, Simon," his mother called.

"Hi," Jenny said, laconically as always.

"Good morning," Simon answered. "Anything new?"

"Not much. It's raining out."

"So I see. Is Earl okay?"

"Sure. He'll be along later."

"Have you had breakfast?"

"There wasn't time. We wanted to get here as soon as we could."

"Well, when you do get something, can you bring some coffee? I can't drink it, but I love the smell."

"We will dear. Give us a couple of minutes."

Simon glowed, causing his shatl to smile. When Clara had been placed in the neurology ward he'd occupied the patient in the bed beside her, a woman who'd been knocked flat by a stroke months earlier. From this vantage point he could hang out with his family, even as he kept an eye on Clara. Given the circumstances, it was a fine arrangement.

A scratching at the window caused his smile to fade. He saw a bird staring into the room. No matter how often it was shooed off, it always came back. The staff had called in pest control and chemicals had been sprayed on the ledge and window. To no avail. Either this bird returned or another just like it. It was as dedicated a visitor as Emma and Jenny. Occasionally it cheeped, as if to say, "You'll never see the last of us."

Simon was frowning now. While the first confrontation with the bolkhs was over, the war was only getting started.

GLOSSARY

Bolkh   creatures that exist in spirit form.

Bolkhin   the language spoken by *bolkhs*.

Domh   the last refuge of the *bolkhs*.

Hamax   a legendary saviour of the *bolkhs*.

Hemindh   a human or animal that has been occupied by a *bolkh*.

Kaba   spirit or soul.

Lakhn   a human soul that is damaged (i.e., drunk, insane, comatose, drugged, etc.).

Limnl   a *bolkh* who has ousted a *lura* baby's soul and permanently occupies his *shatl*.

Lura   the *bolkhin* word for humans.

Shatl   a human body or "vessel."

Smakho   a *bolkh* concoction that intoxicates.

Vadh   an animal body or "vessel."

Vrindh   a mix of *bolkh* and *lura*.

Woplh   the protector of the *hamax*.

Many thanks to Michael Carroll for listening favourably to my pitch about a talking rabbit. And heartfelt thanks to Cheryl Hawley for her close editing of the text and many helpful suggestions. I also owe Sox a huge debt: without his input, there would be no story.

Also by Nicholas Maes

Laughing Wolf
978-1-554883851
$12.99

It is the year 2213. Fifteen-year-old Felix Taylor is the last person on earth who can speak and read Latin. In a world where technology has defeated war, crime, poverty, and famine, and time travel exists as a distinct possibility, Felix's language skills and knowledge seem out of place and irrelevant.

But are they?

A mysterious plague has broken out. Scientists can't stop its advance, and humanity is suddenly poised on the brink of eradication. The only possible cure is Lupus Ridens, or Laughing Wolf, a flower once common in ancient Rome but extinct for more than two thousand years.

Felix must project back to Roman times circa 71 B.C. and retrieve the flower. But can he navigate through the dangers and challenges of the world of Spartacus, Pompey, and Cicero? And will he find the Laughing Wolf in time to save his family and everyone else from the Plague of Plagues?

Locksmith
978-1-550027914
$11.99

Twelve-year-old Lewis Castorman is a master lock-smith: there is no lock on earth that he is unable to open. He is therefore flattered when world-renowned chemist Ernst K. Grumpel invites him to his office in New York City and offers him a lock-picking assignment. His confidence quickly turns to dismay, however, when he learns this job will take him to Yellow Swamp in northern Alberta, the scene of a disastrous chemical spill a year earlier. He is also horrified to discover that Grumpel is utterly ruthless and, through his chemical inventions, can alter the rules of nature at his will. But the assignment is one that Lewis can't refuse.

How is Grumpel able to create such miraculous transformations? What secrets has he locked away and why has he taken pains to store them in Alberta? Despite the strange discoveries Lewis will make at every turn in his adventures, nothing will prepare him for the final encounter that awaits him in Yellow Swamp.

Available at your favourite bookseller.

www.dundurn.com

Visit us at
Dundurn.com
Definingcanada.ca
@dundurnpress
Facebook.com/dundurnpress

Free, downloadable Teacher Resource Guides

teacher resources
www.dundurn.com/teachers

www.ingramcontent.com/pod-product-compliance
Lightning Source LLC
Chambersburg PA
CBHW050026180626
46810CB00002B/589